PUF

GLA

Sam and Seb live in a narrow Edinburgh street which is full of shops selling second-hand things. Their mother, Isabella, sells second-hand clothes, which doesn't exactly bring in a fortune. Money – or the lack of it – is only one of their ongoing problems. As well as the peaks and troughs of the parents' relationship, Seb and his girl-friend, Viola, have a major falling-out, when Seb is suspected of stealing by Viola's parents. And when Sam and Seb's father, Torquil, finally finds a job, he turns out to be working for Viola's father!

Even an eagerly-awaited holiday to the Greek Islands is a disaster in this second collection of stories about Sam and Seb, first met in *Rags and Riches*

Warm, witty and lighthearted, *Glad Rags* also has moments of touching poignancy, which illuminate this story of a lively and endearing family.

Joan Lingard was born in Edinburgh but grew up in Belfast, where she lived until she was eighteen. She is the author of novels for both adults and young people, among which are the best-selling 'Kevin and Sadie' quintet. Joan Lingard has three grown-up daughters and one grandson, and lives in Edinburgh with her Canadian husband.

Glad Rags

Joan Lingard

PUFFIN BOOKS

PUFFIN BOOKS

Published by the Penguin Group
Penguin Books Ltd, 27 Wrights Lane, London W8 5TZ, England
Penguin Books USA Inc., 375 Hudson Street, New York, New York 10014, USA
Penguin Books Australia Ltd, Ringwood, Victoria, Australia
Penguin Books Canada Ltd, 10 Alcorn Avenue, Toronto, Ontario, Canada M4V 3B2
Penguin Books (NZ) Ltd, 182–190 Wairau Road, Auckland 10, New Zealand

Penguin Books Ltd, Registered Offices: Harmondsworth, Middlesex, England

First published by Hamish Hamilton Ltd. 1990
Published in Puffin Books 1992
1 3 5 7 9 10 8 6 4 2

Text copyright © Joan Lingard, 1990
All rights reserved

The moral right of the author has been asserted

Filmset in Palatino

Printed in England by Clays Ltd, St Ives plc

For Neil and Sarah

Contents

Contents

1

A Typical Family Affair

Sam

I'd better start by telling you a bit about our family. It's not a typical family — whatever that is. What I mean is we're not like my friend Morag's family which consists of her and her brother and wee sister and their mother and father. Her father lives at home all the time and has a job with a monthly salary, and they have two coloured tellies, a video recorder, a home computer, a deep-freeze the size of a caravan, a microwave, and a dishwasher.

We don't have many of those things.

In our family there's me, Sam (short for Samantha), and my brother Seb (short for Sebastian) and our father Torquil who comes and goes and is employed off and on (mostly off) and our mother Isabella who runs a second-hand clothes shop in a basement across the road from our flat. As you can imagine, that doesn't bring in a fortune! We have one telly that's on the blink half the time and needs to be thumped to settle down, no video, no computer, no freezer, no microwave. And Seb and I are the dishwashers.

But we do have a granny. And she's certainly part of the family! She lives round the corner.

Well, *normally* she does. But things weren't quite normal at present, as she was staying in our flat to 'keep an eye on us' while our parents were away. Round the corner is a much better place for our grandmother, as far as Seb and I are concerned. Glasgow would be even better since it's more than forty miles from Edinburgh and not even she, with her long-range sight, would be able to see what we were up to from there. But perhaps I shouldn't wish her on Glasgow. I've nothing against the place after all.

Bella and Torquil had gone off to wander round the Greek islands. We'd had postcards from them from all over the Aegean Sea. It looked as if they were lurching about like a couple of drunken sailors, Granny said. They'd been gone for two months and in five days' time we were due to fly out to Athens to join them for half-term. We would then take a boat to one of the islands.

'I think Naxos could be OK,' I said.

OK! The very thought of it thrilled me. You see, Seb and I had never been abroad, unlike everyone else who's been to Spain, Cyprus, Malta, Turkey ... You name it, somebody in my class has been there. I was torn between the islands of Ios and Naxos, was busy studying them on the atlas. Morag had said that Corfu was nice, she'd had a great time there, but it sounded rather hectic to me, with discos going non-stop and lager louts chucking their tins about, and although I like people and lots of things happening, I fancied a bit of peace and quiet for our week's holiday. Our family can make enough noise of its own.

My friends can't believe it when I tell them we usually spend our holidays with our grandfather (on our father's side) in a crumbling old castle in Argyll that's just about to slide into the Atlantic Ocean. Or else we go to visit our giddy aunt, our father's sister Clementina, who lives on an isolated croft in Orkney without any mod cons. And with three utterly exhausting children whom we call the

Flowers of the Field. But more about them later.

Granny goes for her holidays to places like Tenerife
and Ibiza with her friend Etta who works at the news-
agent's. They like to sit by the hotel swimming pool
and sip tequila sunrises.

'Let's get this straight,' Granny was saying now. 'You
are not taking all yon stuff with you!'

And she humphed in the way that only my granny
can humph. My mother says she has it off 'to a fine art'.

'The place is like a midden!' My grandmother was
glaring at the clothes I'd laid out over the backs of the
chairs and on the settee.

You could almost see the hairs standing to attention
at the back of her neck. As a matter of fact you *could* see
them, as she was sitting bolt upright on a hard-backed
chair with a towel round her shoulders, a piece of poly-
thene over the towel, and her head plastered with auburn
dye. Her hair was sticking out in spikes which gave a
kind of porcupine effect. I'd helped with the plastering,
doing some of the bits she couldn't reach.

'Do you hear me, Sam?'

'Yes, Granny.' How could anyone fail to hear her?

'You're hearing but you're not listening.'

Sometimes what she says is true. I kept my head down
and went on studying the map of Greece.

'Look at me when I speak to you, madam!'

'I wish you two would shut up for ten minutes,' said
Seb.

He was trying to do his maths homework. He could
have gone into his bedroom, as I'd already pointed out,
but it would be cold in there and we tend to do everything in the sitting room. Granny was sleeping in it while
our mother was away. We only have two bedrooms.

'One suitcase each,' declared Granny. 'And *no* carrier

bags! I know what you're like, Sam! But I'm not having us look like a bunch of tinkers.'

'That's a racist remark,' said Seb without looking up. He turned the page in his maths book and frowned, the way he does when he's concentrating.

'What are you havering on about now?'

'You're slandering tinkers, Grandmother. Suggesting they're sloppy and untidy.'

I giggled. Granny wasn't sure how to retort to that one so she settled for another humph and shifted herself about. Her chair groaned.

I returned to dreaming about Greece. I could hear a balalaika playing in my head. I could see us strolling through a small white-washed village, finding a taverna with checked tablecloths overlooking the waterfront and eating supper while the sun sank slowly into the dark blue sea, turning it to the colour of blood. The only fly in the ointment was that Granny was coming with us. And she's a pretty big fly.

'Where did you get all those clothes from, anyway?' she was demanding. She's not easily sidetracked. 'Some of them look as if they've come out the shop.'

'I'll wash them when we get home and put them back. Nobody'll know the difference.'

The shop, in Bella's absence, had been left in the care of Granny and myself. My mother likes glitzy clothes made of silks and satins and crêpe-de-chine, tricked out with beads and sequins and feathers. She hates man-made fibres. During the past few weeks polyester trouser suits and 'nice wee dresses', as Granny calls them, had been appearing on the racks in the shop. Granny *likes* man-made fibres. No creasing, washed in a jiffy, drip dry, and Bob's your uncle! Anyone who wants to wear a satin dress that looks as if it's been lying in the bottom of the laundry basket since last Christmas is off their head, as far as she's concerned.

'You've no business taking clothes from the shop, madam!'

The doorbell cut across any further exchange. I went to answer it.

'Don't let anyone in,' Granny shouted after me. 'Unless it's Etta.' Etta is the only one permitted to see her looking like a half-drowned rat.

Our neighbour Mrs Quinn was standing on the landing. She held out a letter.

'This seems to have come through our door by mistake, Sam. I've been out all day, just come in.'

'Thanks, Mrs Quinn.'

'You'll be looking forward to your trip?'

'Oh yes, we are. Very much!'

I looked at the stamp on the envelope. It was Greek. And the handwriting was our father's. My heart did a double backwards flip. It was the first time we'd had a proper letter from them. Surely Torquil wasn't writing to tell us not to come! Or that they'd run out of money — that was always on the cards. The only reason they'd been able to go to Greece was that he'd won a car in a competition and sold it.

I ripped the letter open.

'Greetings, Offspring. I am sitting at a taverna — '

'Who is it?' called Granny. 'There's a draught!'

I thanked Mrs Quinn and closed the door and went back to the sitting room with my eyes skimming my father's handwriting. The letter seemed to be all about the sunset and the wine and the smell of thyme so it seemed that everything was all right.

' "We are very much looking forward to your visit" ' I read aloud. ' "Kindest regards to my one-and-only Main-law. Lang may her lum reek! Love, Torquil."'

'Thinks he's funny,' sniffed Granny, who did not appreciate the bit about her chimney smoking. 'Put the telly on, Sam. We'll catch the news.'

I did as I was told. It had already started. The news-caster was in the middle of saying, 'Air traffic controllers are threatening industrial action ...'

'*What*?' Seb leapt up and came to stand beside me in front of the television.

'Industrial action?' I bleated. I thought I was going to faint.

'They're going to strike!' said Granny grimly, pulling the towel more firmly across her chest.

'St – *strike*?' I felt as if someone was trying to squeeze my windpipe. They couldn't do that to us. They just *couldn't*!

The news-reader, looking us straight in the eye, went on to tell us that traffic controllers were planning to take industrial action as from eight o'clock tomorrow morning, unless ...

Unless pigs flew. Or the moon turned blue. I felt it would take a miracle to sort this one out. Especially when we were due to fly for the very first time in our lives.

'They may *not* strike,' said Seb. 'And anyway, there are five days to go before we leave. Lots could happen in that time. They could go to arbitration and settle it.' He always stays calm, does Seb, never hits the roof or imagines the worst, like me.

I was up at seven the next morning and came into the sitting room to put the telly on before Granny was out of her bed. I had to stop myself laughing when I saw her head on the pillow. It was the worst colour of orange

6

you could ever imagine, sort of singed-looking. With being so bothered about the news we'd forgotten about her hair, and the stuff had got left on too long. You'd have thought it was all my fault the way she went on. 'You were supposed to remind me!'

I put my breakfast on a tray and sat down in front of the telly. As it got nearer and nearer to the deadline of eight o'clock you could see the air traffic controllers weren't going to give in. Heathrow Airport kept popping up on the screen to show gaggles of folk lolling about looking fed up. Who could blame them! I munched my muesli and reminded myself that a lot could happen in five days. Seb had already gone out on the paper round. I'd do the afternoon one. We take it week about and then swop.

Morag chummed me on the round after school. I moaned the whole way. In the *Edinburgh Evening News* it said that neither side in the dispute was making any movement. It sounded like stalemate. Morag wasn't feeling too cheerful, either. They were supposed to go to the Algarve.

I pushed the paper through Viola's door. Viola is Seb's girlfriend. She lives in a posh house in a posh street where no one sells second-hand clothes. They have roses in their front gardens.

As we shut her gate behind us, we saw her coming along carrying her viola case. She waved and we waited till she caught us up.

'It's awful about the air traffic controllers!' she said. 'I hope it won't stop you getting away.'

'Where are you going for half-term?' asked Morag.

'We're driving to France.'

They would be. Her father's a lawyer and her mother's an accountant so they always seem to know the right thing to do. They'd never be destitute or go off to roam round Greek islands leaving Viola in the care of an exasperating relative. They're straight down the line.

Now my parents — as you'll have gathered — step out of line all the time. They're supposed to be separated, yet they can't stay away from one another. Seb says they're like two gases coming together. You know there'll be an explosion eventually. After that they'll not see one another for a bit and then they'll start creeping towards each other again. I know Morag's mother feels sorry for me but you get used to it. We've got used to it, Seb and I. That's just the way it is. And Morag thinks life's far more interesting in our house than her own. Her mum and dad sit in front of the living-room telly every night from six till twelve and don't speak except to say, 'Do you fancy a cup of tea?' 'Wouldn't mind, if you're making one.'

Morag and I hurried on so that I could get home in time to see the news. No change.

Seb's friend Hari was there.

'I wouldn't worry,' he said. 'You remember how last year they were on strike when we were due to fly to India? It was settled the day before we went.'

I cheered up. Yes, I remembered. It had been their first trip back for years.

'Are you wanting to stay for your tea, Hari?' asked Granny. 'It's fish-fingers and beans, mind. None of your fancy stuff.'

Like the fabulous curries his mother makes. Or the pastas and casseroles *our* mother makes. I was missing her. And her cooking.

'I'd like to, thanks, Mrs McKetterick.'

The next three days were agony. I even took my transistor radio to school so that I could listen to the news broadcasts. I got a row for putting it on in French and had it confiscated until after school.

'Well, it's daft listening *all* day,' said Rick. Rick and I are kind of friendly. He and his friend John and Morag and I go round in a foursome. 'It won't solve it any quicker.'

I didn't feel too friendly towards him then! I left him and flounced off. (My granny would say I didn't have red hair for nothing. But Seb has it too and he's slow to rise, though he can when it comes up his back.) It was all right for Rick – *he* wasn't going anywhere. And he's been to Spain and Crete.

There was only a day and a bit to go before we were due to take off. What were our chances of a miracle happening?

When I got in after the paper round that afternoon Seb was sitting in front of the telly with a grin slicing his face in two like a split watermelon.

'It's not – ?'

'It is!'

I was so relieved that I rang up Rick straight away, forgetting all about the row we'd had earlier and that I hadn't meant to speak to him until he'd said sorry.

I packed that evening. Granny was in such a good mood that she didn't go on about the clothes I'd borrowed from the shop or that we weren't to take carrier bags. I could see I would need two at least, though when Morag came round she said they wouldn't let me take more than one piece of hand luggage into the cabin and you couldn't possibly put carrier bags into the hold as they'd spill all over the place when they came round on the carousel. I had a lot of things to learn about this travelling business.

That night my dreams were full of white-washed houses and fishing boats. In one I was out in the boat and being tossed around in a force ten gale. I woke with a start to find I was half-way over the side of the bed. I had thought the Aegean would be calm and blue. I shook my head and blinked. What on earth was that? It had sounded like the doorbell. It went again. It *was* the doorbell.

I pulled on a cardigan and went along the hall in my bare feet. It wasn't seven yet. Too early for the postman. The bell went again, impatiently. What a nerve!

I tugged open the door and gazed into the face of my mother. *My mother!*

'I thought you were never going to come!' she said, tossing her hair (same colour as Seb and me) back over her shoulder. She stepped into the hall, carrying her big green holdall. She looked as if she'd been dragged through a thorn bush backwards.

'I came up from London on the overnight bus,' she said. 'I didn't sleep a wink.'

I followed her back along the hall in a daze.

The bell had got Granny and Seb up too.

'What's going on? Help my kilt! What are *you* doing here, Isabel?' Granny is the only person who calls her Isabel.

'What does it look like I'm doing? I've come home!'

'But you're meant to be in Greece.'

'Well, I'm not. Make me a cup of tea, Samantha, there's a love, and give me a kiss. You too, Sebastian.'

'But where's Torquil?' asked Seb.

'How should I know? I left him in Santorini.'

I was beginning to get the picture. There must have been an explosion.

'So you had a row, eh?' Granny parked her hands on her hips.

Then she and my mother had a row — something *they've* got off to a fine art — with Granny accusing her daughter of thinking of no one but herself, and so on.

'We were looking forward to our holiday! All three of us! We're packed and ready to go.'

'And what was I supposed to do?' my mother demanded. 'Stay with him so that you could come out on holiday? I was worried about getting back in time to catch you before you left. I had to take the cheapest standby flight I could get. I had to come by Air Bulgaria via Sofia. And we were held up for twenty-four hours by some stupid air traffic controllers' strike!'

She made it sound like our fault. At that moment I was fervently wishing that my mother was an accountant and my father a lawyer.

2

A Suspicious Character

Seb

I had never thought of myself as a suspicious character but it seems that that's how some people saw me. It's how Viola's mother and father saw me.

Viola's voice sounded odd on the phone, kind of muffled, as if she had a scarf or something over her mouth. Usually she speaks very clearly.

'Are you all right, Viola? Have you got a cold?'

'No,' she said hoarsely. 'I'm fine.'

'You don't sound it.'

'Look, Sebastian, can I meet you at Henderson's?'

'But I was coming to collect you!' I already had my jacket on, had been about to leave when the phone rang.

'Meet you at Henderson's at seven-thirty,' said Viola very fast and rammed down the receiver. I stared into *my* receiver, then put it back to my ear. But it was dead.

Should I ring her back? No, I thought, better not, she obviously didn't want to talk to me. Or couldn't. Was it because her parents had been listening in? But they'd come to accept me, more or less. I could see that they weren't over the moon about me, as my grandmother would put it, but they seemed to have decided I wasn't as bad as they'd thought at first. I knew they'd have preferred it if my father had been something respectable, instead of – well, instead of a layabout. And one who was at present lying about somewhere in the Aegean Sea.

Viola's mother was always trying to find out what he did for a living. Whenever she gave me the third degree I stuck to my story that he was an actor, which he once had been, for a short while at least, and that he was at present resting. And I'd feel my ears burn round the edges. And I'd be annoyed with him that I'd had to lie on his behalf. Sam doesn't bother. She just says he's hopeless and shrugs it off.

The front door opened, and Sam came into the hall, dropping carrier bags to right and left. Her hair was wet. She'd been swimming.

'What's up with you, standing there like that? Did the cat get your canary?'

I chucked the phone book at her. She ducked. She's good at ducking. The book hit one of Isabella's favourite vases, sending it flying into a hundred smithereens. I had known from the moment I'd heard Viola's voice that this was not going to be my evening.

The noise had brought our mother out of the sitting room.

'What *is* going on here? You'd think you were four years old, the pair of you!' Then she looked down.

'I'm sorry, Bella – '

'*Sorry?*'

'I'll sweep it up and I'll buy you another – '

'Another! It's irreplaceable. How could you, Sebastian, how *could* you?'

Quite easily, I wanted to say, but didn't. Everything was bad enough as it was. I felt like breaking something else. I fetched the brush and shovel and swept up the shards of precious porcelain over which my mother was lamenting, doing her 'Deirdre-of-the-Sorrows' act, as

Sam calls it. She was wringing her hands and accusing me of having no feelings.

'Maudie bought that vase for my birthday five years ago!'

If that was the case it was unlikely to have cost much. Mother's friend Maudie lives from hand-to-mouth, the way we do. She's an aromatherapist, which means that she massages people with different oils, like geranium and peppermint and oregano.

I pitched the remains of Maudie's vase into the bucket and beat a quick retreat.

As I walked up the hill I went back to thinking about Viola and her strange phone call and it occurred to me that she might be going to tell me she didn't want to see me any more. The thought was one I couldn't get rid of. Though the last time I'd seen her we'd had a good time together. We'd walked up Arthur's Seat, the hill that sits right in the middle of Edinburgh, and afterwards gone to McDonald's where we'd met up with Hari and his girlfriend Hilary.

I got to Henderson's at a quarter past seven. I stood at the top of the steps and watched all the people going in. I stamped my feet and put my hands under my arms. You could feel that winter was on its way.

Half past seven came and went. Twenty-five to eight. Twenty to. She was not a girl to make a point of being late. A quarter to. I peered up the street and down the street. And then I saw her. She was running. I went to meet her. Everything was going to be all right!

'I'm sorry, Sebastian.' She was out of breath.

'That's all right, Viola.'

I took her hand and we walked down the steps into the basement café. We lifted trays and joined the queue.

'Do you want anything to eat?'

14

She shook her head.

We bypassed the people waiting for salads and vegetarian hot dishes and went to the end for coffee. We took it into an alcove. I faced her across the table and saw then that she was frowning.

'Is there anything wrong, Viola?'

'Not really.'

'But there is. There must be!'

She fiddled with her spoon, her long dark hair falling over her face, hiding half of it. I felt as if something had got stuck in my throat.

'Can't you tell me?'

She looked up. 'I was thinking perhaps we shouldn't see one another so much.'

We were seeing one another only a couple of times a week, by the time she went to viola and piano lessons and I went canoeing and played rugby and we both did our homework.

'Well, perhaps we're getting too intense,' she said miserably.

'Intense? We just enjoy ourselves.'

'I know.' She sighed.

I began to suspect her mother of using the word 'intense'. I put it to Viola.

'Did she? Is it your parents who're trying to put you off me?'

She didn't answer.

'So they think I'm not good enough for their darling daughter, is that it?'

I scraped my chair back and got up. I felt like picking up the chair and throwing it across the room. Instead, I walked out and headed down the hill, boiling inside like a kettle. I could feel my head rattling like a lid on top with steam building under it.

I went to see Hari.

'You walked out on her? Left her sitting there?'

'She asked for it.' I was beginning to simmer down a little and all I could see was the image of Viola sitting at the table with her brown eyes all bright and shiny.

'Did she? But obviously her parents had been getting at her. Though I wonder why now especially?' Hari looked thoughtful. 'It was a pity you didn't wait to find out.'

I went back up the hill but of course she wasn't there. I rang her from the phone at the back of the restaurant and her mother answered and said 'Just a moment' in a chilly voice and then returned to say that Viola was not available at present. What a muck-up I'd made of everything! I went back down to Hari's. I was beginning to feel like a yo-yo going up and down the hill.

Hari rang Hilary and she rang Viola and arranged to meet her at a café in Stockbridge, near where we live.

'Now you go instead,' said Hari. 'And this time, keep your cool!' He grinned.

Viola and I arrived at the same moment.

'Don't be mad at me, please, Viola! I'm sorry, really I am. I know I shouldn't have walked out on you.'

She agreed to come into the café.

'Now can you tell me what's going on?' I asked.

'I don't know if I can.' Her hair was over her face again. All this was getting me down, and I'm not much good at these scenes, anyway. Sam would have been in her element. Or my mother. They both love a bit of drama, with buckets of emotion.

'It's difficult,' said Viola.

'What is?'

'You wouldn't like it if I told you.'

'I don't like what's going on now. You've *got* to tell me. Please, Viola!'

'Well — OK. But promise you won't be angry with me?'

I promised.

'You know that little antique compass — ?'

'The one on the round table in your sitting room?'

She nodded. 'It's gone.'

'Gone?' I couldn't see what that had to do with me. I'd often picked it up and held it in my hand and admired it. It was a beautifully made compass and I'd said so to Viola's father. Partly to please him. Yes, admit that I'd wanted to please him! He'd told me a bit about it and it had seemed to bring us closer together for a minute or two. So it had gone. So what?

So it began to dawn on me. Slowly. I felt dim-witted. Hari would have twigged immediately. I could feel my ears hotting up.

'You don't mean that *they* think — ?'

'Now, don't explode. You promised, remember! *I* don't think anything.'

'But your parents do, don't they? They think that I — ' I couldn't get the next word out.

'I *know* that you wouldn't — '

'Steal!' I'd said it.

'Of course I know you wouldn't. It was just that the stupid thing disappeared after you'd been in the other afternoon. They didn't *say* you'd stolen it, not in so many words, but I knew they suspected you. They said, "Isn't it odd where it could have gone to? Sebastian was rather fond of it, wasn't he?" Things like that. I turned the place upside-down but I couldn't find it. No one else had been in. I said you hadn't taken it and they said they hadn't said you had. But the next day Mother said she thought we were seeing too much of one another, we were far too young to be getting so intense, and so they didn't want me to go out with you again.'

After all this I didn't see how I could, either. Go out with a girl whose parents think you're a thief?

'Perhaps they've hidden the stupid thing themselves and are trying to frame me.'

'They wouldn't do that, Sebastian. I know they can be pretty awful at times but they've never *lied* to me.'

'Are you sure?'

'I think so,' she said, but she wasn't.

'Most people lie sometime. White lies at least. Unless they're saints.'

And the parents of Viola have no haloes round their heads! Not for the first time I wondered how they'd managed to have a daughter like her.

I wanted to go straight up to their house and defend myself. I wanted to tell them how angry I was. Outraged! But of course they'd be very polite and say that never for a moment had they thought I'd stolen their stupid compass. They'd lie all right. I was in a worse position than if they'd accused me outright.

'I'm so sorry, Sebastian. It's all a terrible mess.'

'You can't help it if you have stupid parents.' I played up the 'stupid'. I wanted to hurt her since I couldn't get at them.

She bit her lip. 'They're not *that* stupid. You've always tended to have a rather stereotyped view of them.'

'Stereotyped?'

'Well, you're always making cracks about lawyers and accountants. They can't all be lumped into one bundle. They vary just as much as – '

'Second-hand clothes dealers?'

'Oh, you can be so stubborn! And prejudiced. Well,

18

you are! You've been prejudiced against my parents from the start.'

'And what about them being prejudiced against me?'

This was getting worse and worse. I thought it was time I went home. I'd had enough.

'You've never given them a chance. Mother's actually quite shy.'

'Shy?' I couldn't believe it. My name for her was Hard-Face. (I didn't use it in front of Viola, of course, though was tempted to then.)

'Yes, she is. I made an effort with your mother, didn't I? I get on with her.'

'Everyone gets on with my mother. Everyone likes her.' And it's true. Isabella's got a way with people. Even though she's a bit zany. But she's warm. And friendly. Which is more than you can say about Hard-Face. When I stand face to face with her I'm frightened I'll get frostbite.

This was crazy! Here we were arguing about our mothers. And we'd never had a row before.

'I wish I hadn't told you,' said Viola. 'I shouldn't have.'

'You had to, didn't you? You couldn't have pretended that everything was OK. Come on, let's go.'

We left the café.

'I'll walk you home.'

'You don't have to.'

'I know. But I will, anyway.'

We said goodnight at the end of her road.

'When will I see you?' she asked.

'I don't know.'

'I'll ring you.' She turned and ran off up the shadowy street. I waited until the sound of her footsteps died away.

I didn't sleep much that night and was up extra early

to go out on the paper round.

'What's got into you?' asked Etta, who had just opened up and was sitting behind the counter, drinking a cup of tea and yawning. She hadn't got the papers sorted yet so I did it for her.

I went up Viola's way first. The street lights were still on. A milkman was walking along the pavement street, whistling softly. The curtains of Viola's house were tightly drawn. I eased their *Scotsman* through the letter box and let it stick there, so that it wouldn't fall into the hall with a thud and waken anyone. The last thing I wanted was the door opening and old Hard-Face standing there on the mat in her dressing gown confronting me. I'd have to get Hari to do the afternoon delivery for me in the future. I would never come along this street in daylight again. You'd think I was a common criminal!

The day in school dragged. I didn't exert myself more than I had to and almost fell asleep in English when the teacher read some poetry aloud to us. She has a soft, lilting voice.

Not long after I'd got home and was making myself a cheese sandwich, the doorbell rang. Everyone else was out so I went to answer it, and who should it be but Viola!

'Oh, Sebastian!' She sounded as if she was about to explode.

'Better come in.'

I took her into the sitting room.

'You'll never guess?'

'They've gone to the police?'

'They've found it. Or rather, Mrs Chisholm — that's our daily help — did. It had slipped down the side of one of the big leather armchairs. Mother and Father are terribly embarrassed.'

'Bully for them!'

'No, but don't you see, they hadn't accused you, so they don't think there's any problem about seeing you again. They even suggested you join us for dinner on my birthday.'

I'd never been asked to dinner before.

'Guilt,' I said, and felt a kind of gloomy satisfaction. Very gloomy.

'Probably. But what I'm asking you to do, Sebastian, is to try to forget what I told you.'

'How can I? I know that your parents suspected me.'

'Oh, it's all my fault. If only I hadn't said anything!'

'But you did. What choice did you have? You had to be honest with me.'

'You don't have to come on my birthday.'

'I don't intend to.'

I was standing by the window. I half put my back to Viola and looked out on to the street. Across the way, in the shop, I could see Bella's red head moving about between the racks of clothes. She always thinks the best of people (well, except for my father, maybe), unlike Viola's parents, who are always suspicious.

'Are we finished, Sebastian?' Viola asked in a tight little voice.

'I don't know.'

'You could at least look at me.'

I turned round reluctantly. Being friends with Hari was a lot easier. If we had a row we always sorted it out quickly. And cleanly.

'Are we going to finish because my parents have been unfair to you? Behind your back.'

'Doing things behind people's backs is worse than to their faces.'

'Oh, all right then! If that's the way you want it.' She moved towards the door. I didn't call her back. I listened to the sound of her feet running down the stairs. The bottom door banged.

I picked up a tennis shoe and threw it across the room. Then I pulled on my anorak. I was going to go round to Hari's and see if he felt like a game of football in the park.

3

A Breath of Fresh Air

Sam

The journey to the Orkney Islands by land and sea is not for the weak, so said our mother, though that did not deter Granny from coming with us, which is what it was intended to do. Bella even got out the atlas to show how the islands sat off the very northern coast of Scotland, a long way up from Edinburgh.

'You don't think *I'm* weak, do you?' Granny enquired.

We couldn't honestly say that we did.

Since we didn't get our holiday in Greece our mother had decided to take us to Orkney for half-term to visit our aunt, Clementina.

'When Clementina asked you to come with us on our next trip you said wild horses wouldn't drag you there,' I reminded Granny. I had a vision of a team of wild horses dragging her across the Pentland Firth, with her riding the waves and crying, 'Mush!' I wanted to giggle but the look on her face told me I'd better not. Also, she doesn't like to be reminded of things she's said when she's changed her mind.

We departed from Waverley Station at 23.25. An unearthly time to depart from anywhere, said our granny. I sat facing Seb, who was in a real black mood. Sometimes these moods come on him and you just have to leave him to work his way out of it: so our mother says. She had her mother across from her which meant that she couldn't stretch out her legs and put her feet on the seat opposite. We couldn't afford sleepers — they'd have cost another eighteen pounds each.

Granny unpacked the food she'd prepared: two thermoses of strong dark tea and a bagful of white rolls filled with slabs of pink boiled ham and bright orange cheddar cheese. Mother declined and nibbled on a healthy fruit and nut bar. Anything with colouring or white flour in it makes her shudder.

'You'll need something more than that to keep you going, Isabel.' Granny thought little of fruit and nut bars and can never understand how her daughter, who was brought up on mince and sausages and steak pies, can have turned into a wholefood freak.

The carriage was far too hot. We hadn't got over the Forth Bridge before Granny was declaring that she was boiling and her feet were swelling. She eased off her shoes.

'That's a mistake,' said our mother, and draped a green silk scarf over her head and face so that it looked as if she was sitting under a lampshade.

The only one who seemed to get much sleep was our grandmother. She snored happily most of the way to Inverness, stopping only briefly when the train lurched and pitched her against Seb, who then had to push her back upright again.

We juddered to a halt at exactly 4.15 am. It was still dark outside except for the gloomy yellow platform lights.

'Imagine,' said Seb, 'British Rail on time! When it wouldn't have mattered if we were a couple of hours late.'

We were not due to catch our connection until 7.10

but when the ticket collector came round he said we could stay on the train until then. He also told us we would be going by bus to Dingwall as the Ness Bridge had got washed away in a flood and hadn't yet been repaired.

'What an uncivilized way to travel,' said Granny, upending the last inch of tea into her cup. 'When you consider that Etta and I can fly to Spain in two and half hours it makes you think.'

'It does, doesn't it?' said Seb. I wondered if he'd had a row with Viola. As far as I knew, he hadn't rung her up to say goodbye, and usually they're on the phone every day to one another. He takes her home and then comes in and rings her up! Rick and I don't get on like that. I couldn't be bothered.

Then Granny tried to put her shoes on and discovered that, while her feet had doubled in size during the night, her shoes had not. She squeezed and groaned but it was no go.

'For crying out loud! What am I to do, Isabel? I can't go in my stockinged feet.'

'I warned you, didn't I?'

'Some sympathy I get from you!'

'Don't start, you two!' said Seb. He decided to go for a walk. I went with him, or rather I ran after him until I'd caught him up.

'Practising for the marathon?'

He grunted.

The air was chilly but refreshing after the steamy heat in the carriage. I glanced sideways at Seb. He was striding up the platform with his arms crossed over the top of his anorak and his head pulled down into his collar.

'Have you fallen out with Viola, or what?'

'We're finished.'

'Finished?'

'*Finito!*' He raised his chin and drew a line under it with the edge of his hand. 'Can you understand that?'

'All right – keep your hair on!'

I wasn't going to get anything out of him. Wringing blood from a stone *would* be easier.

We bought a couple of chocolate bars from a slot machine to give us energy and then went back to see how our relatives were getting on. Granny had solved her feet problem by unpacking her slippers. They were pink quilted satin with pink nylon fur round them, not her style at all. Etta had given her them for her Christmas. Granny had snorted at the time but was glad enough of them now.

We carried our baggage out through the station to where the bus was waiting. On the drive up the coast to Dingwall I noticed that the white caps on the water were looking pretty perky. They'd probably be even perkier on the Pentland Firth, which is much more exposed.

Back on the train again, we chuntered up through some of the wildest parts of Scotland, the Flow country of Caithness and Sutherland. Seb forgot Viola for a while and started on about how people were spoiling the moors by planting trees.

'They're destroying the wildlife's habitats. It's terrible!'

'It's quite disgraceful,' agreed Bella. 'And the government gives people – people that don't even *live* in Scotland, wealthy people – subsidies to plant the trees. It's just a tax dodge for them.'

'I like the look of the trees,' said Granny. 'Yon moors don't do much for me. They're gey bleak looking.'

'It is the natural landscape, Mother,' Bella informed

her icily. 'And we interfere with nature at our peril. As we are beginning to find out.'

But Granny had had enough of nature lessons and had dropped off to sleep again.

We got into Thurso at eleven o'clock, and another bus took us to the ferry at Scrabster.

'You could get to the moon quicker,' said Granny.

As I'd feared, it was blowing a gale on the Pentland Firth. I am not the best of sailors. I began to feel queasy as we went up the gangplank.

I shall skim over the sea journey except to say that Mother and I wondered why we'd ever wanted to come to Orkney at all and Seb felt seedy but didn't throw up. The only person who enjoyed the voyage was our grandmother who bought herself a couple of bacon rolls at the buffet and stood on the deck, feet planted firmly astride in their pink, fur-trimmed slippers, munching them. The rolls, I mean, not the slippers, though she looked capable of eating them, too.

You can't imagine how pleased we were to see the port of Stromness, with its stone houses climbing the hill behind, coming closer and closer! As soon as the boat bumped against the dockside I began to feel better. Mother gave me a swig of ginger ale – it's good for settling the collywobbles.

And there, on the dock, waiting for us and waving, were Donald and Clementina and the Flowers of the Field – Daisy (aged six), Buttercup (four) and Clover (two).

'They're a wild bunch, those three!' said Granny.

We had warned Granny that there would be no mod. cons. but she couldn't get over it.

'Oil lamps in this day and age! An Aga cooker fired

with wood to cook your dinner on! An Elsan!'

The lack of a flush toilet was the last straw and she looked as if she might be about to up and take off. I expect it was the thought of the sixteen-hour return journey that stopped her. At least, I thought, she wouldn't want to come again.

'Not all houses on Orkney are like this,' said Bella. 'Most are fully modernized.'

'We *choose* to live this way,' said Donald.

'I don't blame you,' said our mother, who couldn't exist without the street and her shop and people coming and going. 'I often think we should move to the country and lead the simple life.'

Seb and I looked at one another. Since we'd landed he'd seemed slightly less uptight.

Donald was playing Ride-A-Cock-Horse with the Flowers and there was much screaming and squealing going on. Granny watched with pursed lips. She would love children to be seen and not heard. She's got a point. *Small* children, anyway.

'Such energy,' murmured Bella. 'Can I help you at all, Clementina?'

'No, no, everything's under control.'

Clementina, who doesn't look as if she'd be efficient at anything, is marvellous at cooking and baking, as is Donald himself. They take day about to cook. Granny can't get over that. It fair stumps her!

The smells were fantastic, and the kitchen warm. It's a big, stone-flagged room – the only living room they have – and through the window I could see the black and white cow Gudrun snacking off the grass. Behind her the sky was wide in the way it only seems to be in the Orkney islands, and a soft blue. I could have drifted off to sleep except that I was starving.

On the old scrubbed wooden table Clementina set out a tureen of parsnip soup, home-made bread and oatcakes, a plate of Orkney cheeses and butter, home-made pickles and a big fresh salad which had vegetables from their garden in it and a number of other things which Granny eyed suspiciously.

'Are yon dandelion leaves? Fancy!'

However, she liked the bread and soup and cheese and ate heartily. As did we all. And if Buttercup hadn't spilled her soup into Granny's lap it would have been a peaceful meal.

'They'll wash,' said Clementina serenely, looking at Granny's trousers which, fortunately in this case, were polyester.

'Drip dry and Bob's your uncle!' I said.

My remark was not well received.

Seb and I washed up and then we took the Flowers out for a walk. They clung to us like trailing vines, wanting birlies and piggy-backs and shoulder rides. It was difficult enough walking upright in the wind without a chubby four-year-old weighing you down. You need to be strong to have cousins like ours.

We went down on to the foreshore and spun smooth stones through the choppy waves. The stones were beautiful colours — soft greys and mauves and pinks. I turned each one over to look at it before I spun it.

'They feel good in your hand, don't they?' said Seb. 'They're *so* smooth.'

Thank goodness he was beginning to think that something felt good! The Orkney air must be doing *him* good.

Donald and Clementina's old croft-house sits right on the sea's edge with not another building in sight, except for the grey stone barn where Donald paints and

Clementina designs and makes her fantastic sweaters of every colour of the rainbow. There's not a tree in sight, either. Or a hill. The land goes up to meet the sky. The end of the world, Granny had remarked, looking round on arrival.

It has that kind of feel to it. It's a feeling that Seb and I like – wild and lonely, and as if you've gone back in time. You expect to see the Vikings come looming up out of the sea mist in their curved, prow-shaped boats. The only sounds were that of the wind and the waves and the crying gulls. And the Flowers.

Whenever we wanted to stop spinning and just squat down on our hunkers and watch the sea they jumped up and down demanding, 'Do it again! *Again! Again!*' Their cries merged with the gulls.

I slept like a felled log that night, and in the morning was wakened by a pair of small, cold feet being parked against my warm back.

'Can I come into your bed?' asked Clover, already in and snuggling down. I think she must have stuck her feet in the fridge on the way through – they do have one, run off calor gas. She had with her a large, sharp-edged hardback book which jabbed me in the eye. 'Read me a story, Sammy! I want a story!'

'Read quietly, Samantha,' said my mother and turned over on her mattress, which lay next to mine on the floor.

Granny restricted herself to a humph and also turned over. She had been given the only bed in the spare room. Seb was sleeping in the kitchen. Lucky Seb! Alone, and in the warm! Though he didn't seem to be alone now. It sounded like he was playing Ring-a-ring-of-roses.

I pushed open the door of the barn cautiously. I wasn't

sure if Donald would allow me to come in. He's a big, gentle man but where his work's concerned he can be ferocious. He has to protect his art, Bella says.

'Come in, Sam!'

'Can I?'

'Yes, I'm taking a rest.'

Donald was sitting on a high stool gazing at the large canvas on the easel.

'You can have a look if you want.'

I went to stand beside him. He was painting the foreshore in front of the house and he'd got all the colours bang on and the spray was flying high so that you could almost feel it on your face. It was a bit like being there, only not the same. He hadn't painted it in that careful way where you can see every stroke; it was more or less abstract, yet there was no mistaking what it was meant to be. And there was a terrific feeling of the movement of the sea.

'It's wonderful!' I said. I wished I could explain better how it made me feel inside. But I felt rather shy to try.

I looked round the studio. I loved everything about it: the light, the stacks of paintings, and the painty, turpentiney smell.

'It's all so exciting!'

'Oh?'

'Just – well – everything.'

'Do you like painting, Sam?'

I nodded. I like it more than anything else I do in school. When it's time for art, I can feel my spirits lifting. And as I stood there in Donald's studio I suddenly knew what I would do when I grew up. People are always asking, 'What do you want to do when you leave school?' even though I've got years to go and I usually answer something like, 'I've always fancied working in a chip shop' or 'Rat-catching could be an interesting line to go into.'

I told Donald. 'Do you think I could go to art college?'

'Why not? You've always drawn well, and you've got a good eye for colour.'

I couldn't help feeling a bit puffed up.

'And, Sam, if you really want to do something you must hang on to the idea and not say too much to other people, or let what they say put you off.'

I knew what Granny would say. 'Go to art school! Become an artist? You've got to eat, madam!' She would see me as joining a long tradition of family layabouts. On my father's side, of course. Her family had all worked hard for their living and never had a day off sick in their lives. Granny herself took pride in the fact that even on the day that she was whipped off to hospital with appendicitis she went in to work at the local mini-market where she was manageress. She went in pain. I'm sure the customers would have preferred it if she'd stayed in her bed.

I did talk to Seb. As a brother he can be a right pain in the neck at times but he wouldn't laugh at me for wanting to be a painter. He wants to be an astronomer, and he'd been raving on about the stars you could see up here.

'You won't make much money, of course. It can't be easy being an artist.'

'Unless I become famous!'

'True. Donald's beginning to build up a reputation for himself.'

I sighed, happily. The hassles of the city — how were we going to pay our bills? could the funny smell in the shop be dry rot? where is Father and what would he do when he comes back? — all seemed far, far away.

'I wish we could stay here for three months.'

'So do I.'

'Wouldn't you miss Viola?'

'I told you – it's over. I meant it.'

'What happened?' I could ask him now that he was in a softer, more relaxed mood and the thundercloud had moved away from his face.

He sighed. 'Oh, I don't know. We just seemed to get in a tangle.'

I could understand that. I'd got in a tangle often enough myself and not known how to get out of it.

The week slipped by.

On the last evening we stayed up late. The room was cosy with the golden light from the lamps and the flickering fire. Outside, the wind was howling like a maniac. The smell of woodsmoke was in my hair. I felt dreamy and half asleep. We'd eaten a huge meal and drunk two or three jugfuls of Donald's homemade bramble wine.

'I suppose we should be making a move,' Granny kept saying but nobody did.

In the morning, it was a different story. We had to be up well before first light. Donald put his head round the door to waken us, then retreated. It wasn't long before Granny and Bella started barking at each other.

'We should have gone to our beds early last night,' said Granny, sitting up in bed and giving her head a good scratch. She usually puts in curlers but had been too tired last night. 'When you think of yon journey ahead of us!'

'Nobody stopped you, did they?' said her daughter, before pulling the blankets over her head trying to sneak another five minutes.

I dragged on my clothes and left them to it. We had our last breakfast of porridge and home-made bread. The Flowers were the only ones with much to say.

Donald was to drive us to the boat. We said goodbye to Clementina at the house but the Flowers insisted on being in at the kill and coming to Stromness. Then they wanted to get on the boat.

'Me go too!' screamed Clover.

Donald grappled with her and hoisted her up on to his shoulders. When he bent down to kiss me goodbye, he squeezed my shoulder and winked. Stick to your resolution! he was telling me. I nodded.

Granny held out her hand to him and said politely, 'Thank you for a very nice holiday, Donald.'

'It's been a pleasure, Mrs McKetterick. Come again!'

'You know, Donald, I might just take you up on that!'

Bella groaned, quite distinctly.

Donald and the Flowers stayed on the quay to wave us off.

'Bye, Sammy,' they called, blowing kisses from their plump hands. 'Bye, Sebby!'

'It was a good holiday,' said our grandmother, as the water widened between us and the land and the gulls came wheeling after us. 'I enjoyed it more than I thought I would, I have to say.'

'So did I,' said Seb suddenly.

'But I'll be glad to get back to a proper toilet and the telly. I wonder what's been happening in *Neighbours*?'

4

The Return of the Prodigal

Seb

The last thing we felt like facing after the long journey from Orkney was the return of our father. He wasn't sitting on the doorstep, exactly, that's not his way; he'd gone to the pub on the corner to wait. It was almost midnight by the time our taxi turned into the street — the train had broken down and we'd sat for more than an hour in the middle of the dark Inverness-shire moors until they'd brought a replacement engine.

'Is that not Father?' said Sam, twisting round in her seat to peer out of the back window.

'Torquil?' Our mother came sharply to life.

We all ducked our heads down to look and there, sure enough, standing outside the pub, pausing to take a lungful of night air, was the wanderer, home from the Aegean Sea. Mother says he has a perfect sense of timing — for the wrong time.

'My giddy aunt!' declared our grandmother. 'That's all we need. Drunk and skint, you can be sure of that!'

The taxi was unable to pull into the kerb because of the parked cars, so it stopped in the middle of the street to drop us off. It's always busy, the street, because of the pubs and restaurants and the night club up the other end.

We climbed out, stiff, tired, ready for bed, knowing

35

that there would be no chance of getting there until the wee small hours.

'You get on home, Mother,' said Bella, wasting her breath. You'd think she'd know her own mother by this time.

Our grandmother crossed to the pavement where she stood with her suitcase by her slippered feet. (She'd put the slippers back on when the train broke down, and the heating failed.) She folded her arms. She might be tired but she wasn't going to miss out on anything.

We awaited the prodigal. Isn't it great when it's the father who's the prodigal in the family! After all, it should be me – the *son*! Sometimes I am tempted to take off. Disappear. To London, France, America, or one of the remotest of the Orkney Islands. That sounded like the best idea. Peace and quiet, and a wide open sky. I looked up but could see no stars. It's not easy to see them in the city, which sends up a glare of street lights against the sky.

Torquil came sauntering slowly up the street, stopping to banter a few words with one of our neighbours, Mr McWhitty, who's a joiner, and to whom we have owed money for some time.

'Come on, Torquil,' said Bella in a low, controlled voice. 'We haven't got all night.' I could tell from the mood of her voice that we might be in for a long session.

Torquil came. He saw us. He held out his arms. None of us moved. Sam and I have passed the stage long since of running into his arms, though perhaps he hasn't noticed.

'Sammy old thing! Sebastian! Isabella!' You'd have thought we were a welcoming party.

Then he bowed to our grandmother. 'How nice to see you, Mother-in-law!'

'I don't know that I can say the same for you, Torquil! What time of night is this to be coming home!' There is no point in looking to our grandmother to be logical. She seemed to have forgotten that we had just got home ourselves.

'But where have you all been? I was here at eight, nine, ten – '

'We went to visit *your* sister,' said our mother, making it sound as if we had done it as a favour to him.

'Goodnight, Bella!' called Mrs Quinn, skirting round us with her husband.

'Goodnight!' called Mr Quinn.

We chorused our goodnights and watched them go, arm-in-arm, in through the stair door. Why couldn't our parents be like that? The Quinns have been married for twenty-four years and have never exchanged a cross word, so says Mrs Quinn, though Bella says she doesn't believe that. She says human beings aren't made that way; even the sugar-and-spice ones have a few nasty things inside them squirming around, ready to crawl out at times.

'Let's go in,' I suggested. The whole street would be listening in to us if we stayed there much longer.

Our grandmother came too, which meant that when she did decide to go home I'd have to go out again, to carry her case. Torquil gallantly carried it up the stairs for her.

'So, how was Clementina?' he wanted to know. 'And the Flowers?'

'Spoiled rotten,' answered Granny.

'But sweet,' added Sam.

'They know how to turn on the charm, right enough!' said Granny.

Mother lit the gas fire and we all sat down. In the

light I saw that Father was looking a bit rough, as if he hadn't shaved for a couple of days and had been sleeping in his clothes. His corduroy suit, once blue, now greyish, was bagged and rumpled. But his face and neck were tanned. I had seen him looking worse.

'A cup of tea would be nice,' he said.

'Go and put the kettle on, Sam,' said Bella. 'I need something myself.'

'Why can't Seb?'

'I'll be taking Granny home.'

'Oh, all right!' Sam flounced out.

'So you've been in the pub for the last four hours?' Our mother looked at our father. 'I'm glad you had some money.' (The row in Santorini had been over money. He'd spent, unbeknown to her, most of what they had left, but hadn't been able to say on what. He never could.)

'I only had a half of lager. Or two. The second was bought for me by Sandy Murchie. Nice chap, Murchie.'

Grandmother trumpeted. She thought her daughter had missed out there. Mr Murchie, who often brings presents for our mother, had wanted to marry her, but once Torquil appeared on the scene he hadn't got a look in. Our mother never has known what is good for her, according to our grandmother.

'You took your time getting back from Greece,' said Bella.

'I had to raise the money to get home, didn't I?'

'And how did you do that?'

'I met a man, chap I was in a play with once — '

'And *borrowed* from him?'

'Well, yes — '

'Well, yes! So how are you going to pay him back? You needn't look at me! *I* haven't got any money to spare – the gas and the electricity are due in any day, and I don't get a penny in support for the children, do I? And never will.'

I hate these money rows. I thought of putting on my Walkman but my mother was so worked up that I thought that would probably make her even madder. She was lit up like a torch, and all tiredness seemed to have left her. I think she likes these scenes. Thrives on them, in fact. Her eyes were sparkling and she kept tossing her hair back over her shoulder.

'Mother-in-law – ' Torquil turned to her.

'She hasn't got any money, either.'

'Isabel's right. I'm fair skint after our holiday. It cost a bomb just getting up there.'

'I intend to get a job,' said my father. 'I shall start looking tomorrow.'

'Tomorrow's Sunday,' said Bella.

'Tea,' said Sam, pushing the door open with her foot.

We had a short respite while we drank the tea. Then Bella launched another attack.

'And I suppose you have no money at all on you now?'

''Fraid not.'

'And where do you think you're going to sleep tonight?'

Our father had given up his rented flat when he went to Greece or, more likely, had been thrown out by the landlord for non-payment of rent. I knew where he thought he was going to sleep – in my room.

'Perhaps Sebastian would be so kind as to let me lie on his floor? Just for one night.'

'You can't put him out on the street, Mother,' said Sam.

Isabella looked at her with annoyance before turning back to Father.

'*One* night, Torquil,' she conceded.

By the time I'd walked my grandmother home and gone in with her to check that no burglars had been in in her absence or that Charlie her budgie hadn't died (a neighbour had been feeding him), my father was ensconced in my bed. I had not expected him to lie on the floor. I dragged out a lilo and began to blow it up. It puffed up a bit then deflated with a sharp hiss. It must have a puncture.

'It's good to be home, Seb old son,' said my father, and went to sleep.

In the morning, tired and stiff, I took myself off to Hari's. It was peaceful in the Patel household. They were reading the Sunday papers and drinking tea.

'You could come and stay here till your father finds a place to live,' said Hari. 'You can sleep in the spare room, Mother wouldn't mind.'

I'd have liked to, but if I gave up my room Torquil would settle in and make no effort to find somewhere to live, and Bella would be furious. With both of us.

'But how *is* he going to find a room if has no money?' asked Hari.

'He'll have to find a friend who'll take pity on him.'

When his own family won't. I sighed.

'But you can't let him stay,' said Hari. 'Not if your mother doesn't want him in the house. The flat is not big enough for both of them.'

That was the problem. Now if it had been Grandfather's castle in Argyll then they could have lived in different wings and met up when they were in the right mood.

Father went out round the town looking for friends and must have come across some, for he was away all day and didn't return until midnight. We'd almost begun to think he wasn't coming back when the doorbell rang – Mother won't let him have a key.

'No luck, I'm afraid,' he murmured, with an air of regret.

We went back to school.

It was my week on the afternoon paper round. Hari came with me and did Viola's street. I waited round the corner reading the 'Situations Vacant' columns in the *Evening News*. My eye jumped over them, searching for anything remotely possible. Storekeeper, computer analyst, milk-rounds person, caretaker ... Caretaker!

'How do you see Torquil as a caretaker?' I asked Hari, when he rejoined me. Torquil taking care of anything? It was him that was in need of care.

Hari shrugged.

I suppose, like me, he couldn't see my father as anything but Torquil. Charming, able to talk about every subject under the sun from the tragedies of Shakespeare to the plight of the whale or the price of Guinness, fond of animals and children, and fully-grown people, too, wouldn't harm a fly, would go out of his way not to, would give you his last penny if he had one, though he might borrow it back in the next second, apologetically. That is my father. But he's the only father I've got.

'It's worth trying,' said Hari. 'And it would mean he'd get accommodation as well.'

We'd kill two birds with one stone.

We walked down the hill to Stockbridge.

'I saw Viola,' said Hari.

'Oh?'

41

'She was asking for you.'

'So?'

'You're being hard on her.'

'I've got enough problems in my life.'

'You sound about ninety!'

I gave him a push, but not a serious one. Hari and I have never fought, except when we were seven, over a toy helicopter that we'd each spotted at the same moment lying on the path along by the Water of Leith. We'd both ended up with bloody noses and muddy clothes and the helicopter had got kicked into the river. At that point my grandmother had come along and banged our heads together. For a start, we weren't allowed to go along the Water of Leith on our own when we were seven.

Torquil had come home for the evening meal. I put the ad under his nose.

'Caretaker — for a firm of lawyers!' he read aloud.

A horrible thought occurred to me, but I pushed it down at once. No, coincidences like that couldn't happen.

'I am not sure that I see myself in a legal establishment.'

'There's a basement flat to go with the job. And it's central.'

'Mm, that part of it could be all right.'

'Torquil,' said Bella, as she set a dish of piping hot lasagna on the table, 'go and see about that job!'

He could see that she wasn't going to put up with much more. He raised his hands in surrender.

I went with him to an Oxfam shop and helped him choose a pair of light grey trousers and a checked grey and white tweed jacket.

'Do I look like a member of the respectable Edinburgh bourgeoisie?' he asked the lady, as he emerged from the back room fingering the lapels.

She laughed, which was all she could do. I paid for the clothes from paper-round money that I'd been saving up to buy a telescope with.

'I'll pay you back, Seb old man, don't worry! You're a generous boy. Now shall we go and have a Chinese?' He'd had a win on a horse, enough for a meal. I didn't say that he could have used it to help pay for the clothes. But I enjoyed the meal with him; we get on best when we go off on our own like this. He told me about Knossos, which is the remains of a Minoan settlement on Crete. He made me want to go there.

'One day, Seb, I'll take you – that's a promise!'

The next day, he went for the interview. At two o'clock. As the hands of my watch flickered up towards two, I thought of him standing on the pavement outside the lawyer's office, straightening his tie (his old school one, which Sam had washed and ironed), pulling back his shoulders, stiffening his resolve to go in.

'*Please* go through with it!' I'd begged him that morning, before we got up. '*Please!*'

I couldn't concentrate in Physics.

'You can only do so much, Seb,' said Hari. 'The rest is up to him.'

Hari was right, of course. I nipped in home before going on the paper round. Father hadn't been back. Mother, who was in the shop chatting to a woman in a turban held together by a fake-diamond clip, hadn't seen him.

'If I know him, he'll have been in the pub. *All* afternoon.'

Hari did Viola's street again and while I was waiting for him Viola came round the corner on her way home from school! She was carrying her viola in one hand and her briefcase with her initials embossed on it in the other. That's another thing that marks her out from me – I take my books to school in an Adidas bag, a scuffed one. Why had I ever thought we could get along together?

'Hello, Sebastian.'

I picked myself up off the wall and said hello.

'Why are you avoiding me?'

'I'm not.'

'Then what are you doing standing round here?'

'I don't want to deliver your parents' papers, surely that's obvious.'

'Can't you forgive and forget?'

I didn't see why I should answer that one so I didn't. I looked round the corner and signalled to Hari to hurry up.

Torquil did not come back for supper that night.

'I bet he didn't get the job,' said Sam.

'Or didn't go, more than like,' said our grandmother, who had dropped in. She comes at least once a day to see what we're all up to, as she puts it. She usually comes at mealtimes.

We had fish that evening, which had been given to us – or to Bella – by Mr Murchie. He seems to have connections in the fish business, as well as a few others. He's supposed to be an antique dealer.

'As long as it's not antique fish,' said Granny, and laughed at her own joke.

After we'd eaten, I went out and did a trawl around the streets. I hung about the pub doors, glancing in whenever they swung open, but saw no sign of my father.

I was about to give up when the door of one pub opened and out he came.

'Seb, old son! What are you doing here?'

'I was on my way home.'

He fell into step beside me. 'I was just about to come home myself. I'd only nipped in for a quick drink to celebrate – '

'*Celebrate*? You mean, you *got* the job?'

'I did, indeed. They offered it to me on the spot. They took to me straight away. I could see that in the first five minutes. There were three of them. The senior partner and I were at school together. He spotted the tie. Good idea of Sam's.' (He hadn't wanted to wear it; he loathed anything to do with 'old school ties'.) 'Yes, we had a long chat, Hector and I, about the old days and that kind of thing, and he said he was sorry I had fallen on hard times and would like to help me.' Then Torquil told me Hector's surname.

The horrible thought I'd had before he applied had come true. It looked like my father was going to work for Viola's father.

5

Employing Granny or
Keeping Granny off Mother's Patch

Sam

'We'll have to find a part-time job for your grandmother,' said our mother. (Note how she said '*your* grandmother' and not '*my* mother'.) I think Torquil finding a job had put the idea into her head.

I murmured; Seb didn't respond at all. He was holding a bag of frozen green peas over one eye and trying to read with the other. Someone had jabbed him in the eye with an elbow at rugby: that was his story, and he was sticking to it, to Bella, at least. I knew differently.

'I can't stand having her on my patch all day long, day in, day out,' our mother went on. 'She's driving me crazy!'

She was exaggerating, of course, though Granny did trundle down the steps of the shop at some point every day. When the light suddenly became blocked off in the shop, we'd know she was coming. We'd look up and there she'd be, peering in through the window, trying to catch us in the middle of something we shouldn't be doing. Then she'd descend the last two steps, complaining about the bottom broken one and telling us we'd be sued if a customer broke a leg falling down it.

'An interesting thought – a broken leg,' our mother had been heard to murmur, eyeing her mother's two stout legs, planted firmly astride in their polyester trousers, as she took up the middle of the floor and surveyed the scene. Then Granny would pounce.

'What in the name is this, Isabel?' she'd say, holding up a garment between her finger and thumb as if it might bite her, before letting it drop to the floor.

'The trouble is she hasn't enough to do.' Bella glanced sharply at Seb. 'How's your eye?'

'All right.'

'Let's have a look!'

With a sigh, he lifted the packet of peas which by now had defrosted, anyway. He was going to have a beezer of a black eye.

'Honestly, Sebastian! I wish you wouldn't play that dreadful game. It's downright dangerous. You were lucky you didn't get your skull fractured.' She went over to examine him close up. 'I'm sure Maudie would have something for it. I'll give her a ring.'

Maudie came over and daubed arnica lotion on it. 'It's magic,' she said. 'You'll see! Arnica's great for taking the pain and swelling out of bruises.'

Granny sniffed. (She had arrived in just before Maudie.) She doesn't hold with Maudie's 'rubbish ideas'. A lump of raw steak would be better, in her opinion.

'We can't afford steak,' said my mother tartly. 'We're broke.'

'No use looking at me, Isabel.'

'I was not looking at you, Mother.'

'I could be doing with a few extra bob myself.'

Bella had her opening. 'I was thinking you might enjoy having a little job again, Mother, something to occupy you for a few hours a day.'

'I'm enjoying my retirement, thanks very much. Now I can do what *I* like.'

She had been indignant when she'd been compulsorily

retired at the age of sixty-two. She was just getting her
second wind, she'd told the man who owned the mini-
market, but he'd wanted the job for his nephew. She'd
tried to get something else then, without any luck. She
was too old for supermarket check-outs and the Pakistani
shops round about tended to employ their own relatives.

'You still have a lot of energy, Mrs McKetterick,' said
Maudie.

'You're right, Maudie. I do!'

Seb slid out while they were discussing Granny's
energy level. I followed him to his room.

'You didn't get that at rugby, did you?'

He shrugged.

'It's all over the school.'

'As long as it's not all over this house.'

'I won't tell.'

Seb had been in a fight, and if our mother knew she'd
hit the roof. The fight had been over Hari. Most of the
time Hari's left alone, but when anyone harasses him he
copes by restraining himself and keeping his dignity,
which Bella says is the best way. His build is slight,
whereas Seb is what Granny calls 'well-built'. That means
he's got wide shoulders, which are good in a rugby
scrum. And he's hotter-tempered than Hari so sometimes
when Hari's under attack he'll let rip. As he had that
day. Two yobs – two real troublemakers – called Billy
Clarke and Len Wilson had been having a go at Hari,
calling him a darkie, telling him to go wash his face.
Infantile! Bella would call it. But I could understand Seb
lashing out. If I could arrange to put a banana skin in
the path of those two yobs, I'd do it.

Maudie was right about the arnica: it did work wonders.
By supper-time the next day the bruise was going down

rather than coming up and it was hardly sore at all, Seb said. It was a pity Clarke and Wilson couldn't be put down as easily. They'd been rumbling again that day in school.

Our mother was poring over the 'Situations Vacant' column in the *Edinburgh Evening News*. There's no stopping her once she gets a bee in her bonnet. I hung over her shoulder.

'Office cleaner?' I pointed to an ad.

'Don't be ridiculous! As if I'd let my own mother go out and clean offices!'

'It's half-six in the morning, anyway,' said Seb, who was reading another copy of the paper. 'Till eight thirty. That'd leave her plenty of time to come in afterwards and annoy you.'

Bella is seldom out of her bed before half past eight. She prefers to wait until after Seb and I have gone out to school; she says she can't stand the frantic way we rush around looking for things we should have found the night before. So when the door thuds shut for the last time she emerges from her cocoon and eases into the day, as she calls it, drinking herb tea and reading the *Scotsman* in her dressing-gown. It isn't worth opening the shop before eleven.

'The ideal thing would be a few hours a day doing light housework and shopping for some elderly person. Your grandmother would love to have someone else to boss around, and she adores shopping.'

But there was nothing to fit the bill.

When Mr Murchie came by with a pound of herring, Bella asked if he couldn't use some help in his antique shop.

'To keep the shop for you while you go to sales? To do the dusting, polish the brasses? We're looking for some sort of employment for Mother.'

But Mr Murchie closes the door and hangs up a notice when goes to sales – like most folk in the street – and he doesn't bother much with dusting.

'I'd take her on if I could, Isabella. But my profit margins wouldn't allow it.'

Bella went back to studying the 'Situations Vacant'. Seb said she was wasting her time; Granny was in no mood to take a job even if one was found for her.

Then Etta got the idea of going to Morocco for a week after New Year.

'It'd be nice and warm there in January. And it'd make a change, with the desert and camels and palm trees and all that. We could go for day trips.'

'On a camel?' I asked.

'You never know!' Etta gave me a wink.

Granny quite fancied going, too, after she'd sniffed and humphed a bit and said she wasn't sure about going to *Africa*, but after she'd looked at the brochure and seen that the hotels looked just like hotels did anywhere and that they had swimming-pools and poolside bars, she began to come round to the idea.

'I wouldn't mind a week away in January, I must admit. But it's not on, Etta. I just can't afford it, not on my pension.'

'You could take a job, Granny,' I jumped in quickly. 'A part-time job.'

'And how am I to get one, madam? When folk are being tossed on the scrap heap at fifty these days!'

'We've been looking,' I began and quickly changed it to, 'We'll look.'

I'd had an idea. I went to see Mrs Quinn.

'There wouldn't be a job going serving dinners at your school by any chance?'

'As a matter of fact there might be, Sam. One of the women's been off for ages and we don't think she's coming back. I'll have a word with the supervisor.'

Mrs Quinn works in a local primary school. I thought it would suit Granny down to the ground (as she would say) to be a school dinner lady. She'd have plenty of scope for bossing; she could keep the kids in line and tell them not to push or shove and to eat up their greens or they'd turn purple in the face or their hair'd fall out.

Mrs Quinn rang our bell next day. Her supervisor had said that Granny should come and see her if she was interested in the job.

'Fantastic! Thanks a million, Mrs Quinn.'

I went to put the proposition to Granny.

'A job serving school dinners?' She sat in her chair with her feet on her footstool, a wee glass of port on the table beside her, and considered. She'd been watching telly when I came in, like a lady of leisure.

'You want to go Morocco, don't you, Gran?'

'I don't know that I should let Etta go on her own, that's the thing. She's got no sense of direction.'

'She could get lost in the desert.' I could imagine Etta galloping across the desert on a camel, hanging on for grim death, and disappearing into a cloud of dust.

Granny eyed me and I gazed back, innocently; or at least I hoped I was looking innocent. 'I hardly think anyone'd let Etta loose in the desert on her own.'

I picked up the brochure, which had been lying beside Granny's chair. 'It looks fabulous, doesn't it? Look at that minaret! I'm sure you'd love it.'

And you never knew what she might come home with. A sheikh, maybe? Last time, when she and Etta had gone to Tenerife, it had been a butcher. They'd had a short romance which finished when Granny got tired

of cooking him mince and chops. She'd opted for inde-
pendence.

'You'd probably quite enjoy dishing out the dinners.
I mean, it's not *terribly* hard work, and primary kids are
easier to keep in line than secondary.'

'You're telling me!'

She swithered, drank her port, swithered some more,
and finally agreed to see the supervisor. She put on her
best suit and went the next day.

'Well, I've got the job,' she announced, when she
came in at supper-time. 'I start tomorrow.'

'This calls for a celebration,' said Bella, and opened a
bottle of fizzy wine which Mr Murchie had brought her.

The next day Morag and I decided to have school
dinners. We only have them now and again. Sometimes
we take sandwiches with us, or else we go to the chip
shop and buy chips or bits and pieces (chocolate biscuits,
crisps, all things that Bella disapproves of). We were
feeling cold that day and wanted something hot, and
Morag's mother had been giving her a row about eating
too many chips and bars of chocolate. She'd said that
was why Morag had so many spots. I wasn't crazy about
having spots either so I'd made a resolution, too, to eat
less rubbish.

Rick and John came with us. We each took a tray and
joined the queue. There was fish pie which didn't look
too bad. We were all so busy gabbing that I didn't notice
that it was our turn to be served.

'Come on, get a move on, I haven't got all day to
stand here!' The voice boomed over my head. A very
familiar voice. I couldn't believe it! I turned round to
stare in the face of my granny, who was wearing a white
overall fastened with tapes across her chest and a white

hat stuck on top of her auburn hair. In her right hand she held a scoop.

'Granny!' I gasped. 'What are you doing here?'

'When I got along to the primary I found the other woman had turned up. So the supervisor said they were needing extra help here.'

It looked like we'd managed to move our grandmother off our mother's patch on to our own!

'I'll be able to keep an eye on you all now,' said Granny, as she ladled out my portion of fish pie.

Morag and I didn't go to dinners for a few days and then came a wet and windy morning when we didn't feel like going out. I would have taken on the wind but the boys and Morag wouldn't be budged.

'Oh, come on,' said Rick. 'Your gran can't eat you.'

'No, but she might eat you instead!'

'I'll risk it!' He grinned. He always makes a point of chatting to her and she thinks he's a nice lad!

We ended up behind Seb and Hari in the queue. They turned round to talk to us, seemed positively pleased to see us. Relieved, almost, I might have said. And then I noticed the two boys in front of them. They were Clarke and Wilson.

Clarke was bumping his tray up against Hari's and sniggering.

'Grass eater, are you?' asked Clarke, eyeing Hari's plate of salad, before bumping his tray again.

Hari put out his hand to stop his plate from sliding off and accidently touched Clarke's tray.

'Take your dirty hands off my food!' said Clarke. I should have said 'snarled'. He reminds me of a Rottweiler.

'He didn't touch it,' said Seb.

'I'm not going to eat food that a wog's put his dirty mitts on,' yelped Clarke.

'Look at the colour of them!' said Wilson. 'Shit-brown.' Then the two of them doubled over as if he'd said something funny. Ha, ha! The rest of the queue had gone silent and I could feel my mouth drying up.

'Belt up, both of you!' Seb took a step towards them, but Morag and I grabbed him and held him back.

'It's all right, Seb,' said Hari quietly, touching him on the arm. 'They're not worth bothering about.'

'You lot should be sent back to where you came from,' said Clarke. 'Chimpland!' And he did a little ape-like dance and scratched his head as if he had nits. Probably did, too. Come to think of it, he looks a bit like an ape himself.

Meanwhile, the queue was getting restless behind us and so was Granny, who was waiting with her scoop. She'd already put out two plates of lentil soup for Seb and Hari and set them on the counter. She knows they're fond of lentils.

'Move up!' she barked.

Clarke moved backwards, keeping his face to us. He did another ape-like jig, and the next thing happened so fast that we couldn't properly make out what *had* happened until afterwards. One of the plates of lentil soup that Granny had set out had either been knocked accidentally — or deliberately? — off the counter, and the soup had gone all over the floor. Clarke lost his balance on it and went flying on to his back with his trayful of meat and veg. His back was covered with lentil soup, his front with Irish stew. The whole dining-room collapsed into laughter, cheers rang out, spoons were banged on the table. Clarke is popular only with fellow yobs.

When he got back on to his feet, scrambling to get his balance, more gales of laughter broke out. He looked a right idiot. He slithered away with his head down, glancing neither to left nor right. Wilson lurched after him in his spiked boots, trying to look jaunty and as if he couldn't care less. About anything. He wasn't convincing. A chorus of jeers helped them on their way.

One of the other dinner ladies came out with a mop and began to clean up the floor.

'Move along then!' ordered Granny. 'We'll never get done at this rate. Do you think I've nothing else to do but stand here all day?'

Seb and Hari were served, then it was my turn.

'Lentil soup,' I said. 'Please!'

My grandmother ladled it out and passed it over.

'Thanks, Gran.'

'There's nothing to beat a good bowl of hot soup on a cold day,' she said, with a gleam in her eye.

6

Taking Care

Seb

When I'd realized that Viola's father was the solicitor that *my* father was going to work for, I'd just about collapsed in a heap on the floor.

'Aren't you pleased then, Seb?'

'Well, I — I don't know. Are you sure you *fancy* a job like that?'

'What do you mean "fancy"? It's a job, isn't it? That's what you said to me. And it's a good-sized flat. There'll be plenty of room for you to come and spend week-ends with me. The rooms are big, too. We could have a party.'

'I don't know if you should do that.'

'What? Have a party? Why ever not?'

'The lawyers might not like it.'

'They'll have gone home by then.'

I knew that if my father were to have a party it would be the night Viola's father would return to the office to collect some papers. My father has the knack of attracting trouble.

He had a week before he was due to start so he took himself off to Argyll to visit *his* father. I chewed things over with Hari, wondering what I could do to get myself out of this one.

'You can't really do anything, can you?' said Hari.

'But can you see Torquil taking *care* of a four-storeyed building?'

'You encouraged him to apply.'

'I know. I was desperate.' I'd wanted my bed back, which Hari agreed was not an unreasonable thing to want.

Torquil returned from the west in good spirits. Hari and I helped him move into his new flat. It didn't take long; he only has a few bits and pieces. It was Sunday, so there was less chance of Viola's father being around. They go out in the car for runs in the country at weekends and have lunch at a restaurant. Viola says that since her parents are both very busy during the week they make a point of keeping the weekend for the family. But, even so, I had a good look up and down the street when we went in and out.

The office was in the West End, in a terraced Georgian block. The buildings had been built as houses but were now mostly too big for people to live in so they'd either been turned into offices or broken up into flats. We did a tour of the building and were easily able to pick out Viola's father's room. It was the biggest, and had elaborate cornices and a smooth carpet on the floor; and sitting on the desk was a silver-framed photograph of Viola and her mother. They were both smiling. I glanced away.

'Hey, look – here's Viola!' Hari picked the frame up.

'Don't touch it!' He'd leave his fingerprints on it. I felt as if a secret spy camera was watching us.

'Nice looking girl,' said Torquil.

'Yes, she is,' said Hari.

'Do you know her?'

'No,' I put in quickly. I didn't want *my* father telling *her* father that I knew her.

Hari smiled, and replaced the photograph.

We went back down the stairs. The main staircase had wrought-iron banister rails and a cupola overhead that let in light. Our voices echoed in the stair-well.

The basement flat would probably have been the servants' quarters originally. There were four rooms, half-furnished with fusty furniture, and an old-fashioned kitchen with a white porcelain sink stained green under the taps, and a greasy gas cooker. Torquil was unlikely to do much cooking. At the back the flat opened out on to a patch of scrubby grass and a car park. Behind that ran a lane.

The rooms smelt stale. We pushed up the heavy windows and let in some air. They were all barred.

'Bit like being in jail,' said Torquil cheerfully.

In the corridor, opposite the kitchen door, was the safe, a big, black, solid-looking affair.

'The crown jewels,' said Torquil, saluting it.

I wondered what they would keep in it. Petty cash, I supposed, and important documents, ones that couldn't be stacked with the others in the shelves upstairs.

'What do you have to do, Torquil?' asked Hari.

'See that burglars don't break in, that kind of thing. They've given me a big flashlight, like a searchlight! And I have to let the cleaners in in the morning.'

'At what time?' I asked.

'Six.'

'Six o'clock in the *morning*? You'll never be up!'

'They'll ring the bell, won't they?' My father was in the kind of mood that nothing seemed to dismay him. Sometimes he's in the opposite mood. He swings up and down like a pendulum. It's one of the things that my mother says she can't cope with.

We had a cup of coffee, then left him to get on with his caretaking. It was a terribly big, cold place to live in all alone.

'But he'll only live in his small part of it,' said Hari, who's always got a sensible answer. 'He'll live in one room.'

I thought that Torquil probably wouldn't last more than twenty-four hours, that our bell would ring and there he'd be on the landing mat, his bags at his feet, asking to be let in. But two days passed, then three, and four, and he didn't come. I rang him up, and he said everything was fine.

'No problems, Seb. Come and see at the weekend.'

I went on Sunday, going in by the lane and banging on the back door. He opened up, looking sleepy and unshaven. He'd had a late night.

'Are you allowed to go out at night?'

'I can't stay in all the time, can I?'

I supposed not.

'I set the alarm when I go out. Anyway, getting in here would be like getting into Fort Knox.' The front and back doors both had two locks and a bolt, as well as a chain.

Torquil shaved, and we went for a walk on Arthur's Seat. From the ridge you can look down on the whole city and see its streets and gardens laid out, and its spires and towers sticking up, and the Firth of Forth and the Kingdom of Fife beyond. I had often walked on the hill with Viola. But I hadn't come up here to think of *her*. I was doing my best not to think of her at all these days.

When we came back down into the Queen's Park, Torquil said that the cool fresh air had done his head a power of good. Saying goodbye, I felt better about him than I had for a while. He seemed to be coping.

So when, two or three evenings later, the policeman came to our door, I was startled. He asked for Torquil.

'Who is it?' my mother called from the living-room. She'll never answer the door herself, yet she wants to know who's there the moment you open it.

'You'd better come in,' I said to the constable with resignation. If there was trouble in the offing, I wasn't going to handle it on my own.

'Don't tell me the shop's been broken into!' said Bella, the moment the constable came into the room. Shops and flats are broken into along the street all the time. And we don't have such a thing as a burglar alarm; we can't afford one.

'Not as far as I know, madam.'

Sam lifted a pile of clothes so that he could sit down. 'It's the legal premises your husband looks after.'

'What are you doing here, then?' asked Bella, frowning, and running her fingers through her hair.

'Looking for your husband, madam.'

'But how did you *know* to look for him here?'

'The couple that look after the property next door to the lawyers told us he was married to you. Said you ran a second-hand clothes shop in the street here.'

'Big Mouth,' said Bella, meaning Torquil. He could never resist telling his life story.

'Have you seen him this evening?'

'I haven't seen him for a week!' my mother answered haughtily. 'And we know nothing about any break-in.'

I asked what had happened, and the constable filled us in with the details. Around nine o'clock, apparently, the thief, or thieves, had forced an entry by prizing open the bars on the kitchen window.

'Easy enough to do with a jemmy. They were obviously professionals.'

'But didn't the alarm go off?'

'It hadn't been set.'

There was a pause while we all considered that.

'Dad must have forgotten to set it before he went out,' said Sam.

'Trust Torquil!' Bella shook her head.

'Anyone could forget,' I said quickly.

'Wasn't it funny though,' said Sam, 'that it should be the very time when the burglars tried to break in?' She stopped, and realizing what she had said, turned scarlet.

'Yes, we thought it odd, too,' said the policeman.

Torquil was in a pub, as one would expect. He spends a lot of time in pubs, not because he drinks all that much, but because he likes to play darts and dominoes and talk to people. He likes company, and noise and warmth round him. I tracked him down and told him the news.

'Oh, Lord! What a blithering idiot!' He struck his forehead with the palm of his hand. 'I was going to put the damned alarm on and then the phone rang and after I'd answered that I forgot all about the alarm.'

I went with him to the police station and waited in the outer office while he was being interviewed. I knew that they'd be grilling him, that one of the things they'd be considering would be that he had left the alarm off deliberately and then tipped off the thief. The constable had had a good go at my mother and Sam and me; questioning each of us in turn, wanting to know if we had been to the premises, and how often. He had written everything down in a notebook. I'd felt myself getting hot around the collar and I'd remembered how we'd left fingerprints in some of the upstairs rooms. Hari's were on Viola's picture. But there must be masses of finger-prints all over the place. And there was no way that they'd suspect Hari. But it's awful how you can start feeling guilty when you've not got anything to be guilty about.

Bella became annoyed with the policeman in the end.

'Go ahead,' she'd said, 'search the flat, take it apart, see if you can find any stolen goods!'

'I'm only doing my job, madam, following up all lines of inquiry.' He'd put his pen back in his pocket but had not taken her up on her offer.

I sat under the harsh yellow lights in the police station and thought about the burglary. The thief had blown the safe door open. It had been a controlled explosion — the building hadn't been damaged. The sound would have been muffled but had been heard by the couple next door, who are professional caretakers and have an ear for suspicious noises. Hearing that one, they went round the back to investigate and saw that the bars of the kitchen window had been pushed apart. They'd rung the police, but the thief had worked quickly and by the time the squad car was on the scene he'd scarpered, with the contents of the safe. It was likely he'd had a mate waiting with a car in the back lane.

Of course it could just have been a coincidence that the burglars arrived on the scene on the evening that the alarm had not been set. But tell that to the marines! — as my grandmother would say. Or to the police.

My head jerked up, and I looked around, wondering where I was. I must have fallen asleep. The clock on the wall said one. I'd never get up for school in the morning, and we were having a maths test.

Then Torquil appeared. He looked bleary-eyed, and although he said in a bright enough voice, 'Come on then, Seb old son, let's go,' I could see that he was not cheerful underneath.

We walked down the road together. A chill wind had sprung up and was whipping the dry leaves along the street. I put up the collar of my anorak and pushed my hands deep into my pockets.

'You'll never guess, Seb, but I believe they think I'm involved! Can you imagine anything so crazy? I'm not though, you know. You do know that, don't you?'

Yes, I did, for whatever faults he might have, I was sure he was honest.

I rang home and told Bella I was going to stay the night with him.

I got up at six when the cleaners rang the bell. The police had told Torquil not to let them touch anything so I sent them away, then went back to bed again and was wakened a couple of hours later by a man's voice calling Torquil. I scrambled up, grabbing my jeans from the floor, and came face to face with Viola's father in the corridor.

'Sebastian! What are *you* doing here?'

I explained.

'I didn't realize you were his son.'

'Well, I am,' I said, and looked Viola's father straight in the eye.

He turned his attention to the half-demolished safe. He sighed.

'We are insured, of course, but some things can never be recovered.'

I wondered what kind of things he was talking about. He went on to tell me that all his family's valuables had been in the safe, heirlooms which had been in the family for a hundred years and more, diamond and ruby brooches, emerald rings, stuff like that.

It was not long before the police returned. They

wanted to go over the details of my father's movements yet again.

I went for a walk on Arthur's Seat to try to clear my head. School wasn't going to see me that day; I had more pressing things to get on with. Bella would have to write me a note to cover my absence.

I thought of my father going to the pub, talking to people. I remembered Bella calling him 'Big Mouth'. It's true that he does tell people too much, but it comes from being so keen to have their company. I could imagine him saying, 'I've got this job, in a big lawyer's office ...' I thought of the people he might talk to – all kinds of people. Some of them could be criminals: house-breakers, safe-breakers. There are so many of them around these days that it was perfectly feasible. They might see him regularly in the pub. They might have got the idea that when they *did* see him in the pub then the coast would be clear at the lawyer's for a break-in. They could buy him a few drinks, keep him occupied.

I ran back down the hill and jumped on a bus that took me to the West End.

My father was sitting in the kitchen looking dejected.

'Torquil, have you told anyone sort-of-suspicious-like in the pub about your job here?'

'Don't *you* start, Seb! I've had enough.'

'No, but listen!' I told him what I'd been thinking.

'But I didn't tell anyone I hadn't put the alarm on.'

'I know that. That could just have been a coincidence. After all, thieves do break in where there are alarms. Professionals must know how to put them out of action.'

'I'm tired, Seb.'

'Think about it! Think about the people who came into the pub you were in that night.'

He thought. Then he said slowly, 'There *are* one or

two men who might be termed "shady characters". But, on the other hand, they might not have had anything to do with it. I wouldn't like to accuse anyone without good reason.'

'Did they buy you a drink that night?'

Yes, he admitted, they had. More than one.

'Torquil, if there's any chance they could be involved you'll have to tell the police.'

'But if it is one of them then it *will* have been my fault! For telling them where I worked.'

I thought of Viola's father and what he would think of me when he knew that my father had caused him to lose his family heirlooms — through shooting off his mouth.

'You made a mistake, Torquil. But it's not a crime.'

'No, it isn't, is it?' he said unhappily.

'And if they catch the men quickly, they might get the stuff back.'

I went with him to the police station again. He disappeared into the back room to emerge an hour later, looking washed-out but relieved.

'I think I did the right thing, Seb. I picked out the two men from photographs on police files. One of them is a well-known safe-breaker!'

'Maybe you shouldn't go back into that pub again?'

'Maybe not.'

We stopped off for a cup of coffee and a sandwich. Neither of us had eaten that day.

'And now I think I'd better go and tender my resignation, don't you, Seb? And 'fess up there!'

I sat in the kitchen downstairs while he went up and talked to Viola's father. All this sitting around waiting was making me edgy. I kept getting up and down to look out of the window, but there was nothing to see except the cars parked on the back lot and the wind ruffling the coarse grass.

When Torquil came back down he said that his resignation had been accepted. They had both agreed that perhaps he was not terribly suited to the job of caretaking. I couldn't really disagree.

'We shook hands on it, though.'

At least that was something.

7

Stocking Up

Sam

Running a second-hand clothes shop isn't like running an ordinary shop where you choose stock from catalogues or a rep calls and you put in your order. Keeping the stock up means searching for it, being out and about. Which suits me.

After my mother had returned from the Greek islands, she threw out half the things that Granny had bought in – all the polyester dresses and 'nice wee suits' and sensible button-up-to-the-neck-no-nonsense cardigans. Granny was furious.

'You never did know what side your bread was buttered on, Isabel!'

'I have my own clientèle and they expect me to stock a certain *kind* of garment.'

'Clientèle!' Granny sniffed. 'Is that how you cry them? Bunch of deadbeats, if you ask me! I was building up a nice line of customer for you, folk who've got sense, as well as money to pay for what they buy.'

Often Mother's customers don't, and have to ask for 'tick'. Most of them pay up eventually, although there are one or two who never seem to have it on them and say, 'Next time, Bella! I promise. I won't forget …' And they drift off up the steps looking vague and with something else under their arm.

We didn't actually throw out Granny's purchases; we packed the lot into carrier bags and Morag and I lugged them down to the Oxfam shop. They let us have a few things for half-price in return — two or three satin blouses and a couple of evening dresses with low backs and sequined tops. I know the women in all the charity shops in Edinburgh. Morag and I tour round them on Saturdays.

Our other haunts are jumble sales. In the weeks leading up to Christmas there are two or three on every Saturday in some church hall or other. Morag and I arrive well before opening time to make sure of a place at the head of the queue along with the other dealers. You need sharp elbows for this game and you have to be quick on your feet. Morag and I can outrun the dealers and we know exactly what we're looking for. When we see anything glitzy we grab it. It's great when you get a bargain — we come home feeling dead chuffed with ourselves.

But the best finds are usually in people's houses, old people's houses. Often they've stored stuff for years in trunks and boxes and they decide to have a clear-out, or they're moving to sheltered housing where they'll have less space. Or sometimes it's because they've died, which is not so much fun. None for them at all, of course! But I don't like it much myself — it feels kind of creepy to be going through dead people's clothes, so usually I let my mother go on her own.

But one old person's house we hadn't thought of looking for stock in was our own ancestral home. Grandfather's castle in Argyll.

He had rung up to see if Torquil had any money left from his competition win.

'You must be joking,' said Bella. 'And he's just lost

his job.'

Grandfather was desperately in need of money. Well, what was new? And who wasn't? Apart from Morag's father who's in Marketing and is sharp when it comes to figures. Their family's run on budgets. Morag had tried to get us organized but we don't have enough regular money coming in to budget, so she gave up on us.

The roof of the castle was in a terrible state and had been for years; that was what Grandfather wanted money for. Whenever we went and it rained (which it usually did), Seb and I spent half our time on drip detail, trying to put the buckets in the right places, emptying them before they overflowed. We never asked how Grandfather got on when we weren't there. He certainly couldn't climb into the roof-space.

'And I'm sorry,' Bella was saying into the telephone, 'but I can't possibly do anything, either.' She listened. 'Mother? Oh, no, she's only got a little job now — it helps keep her in port and chocolate. And she's going to Morocco. It would take a fortune to mend that roof, though I suppose you're only thinking of patching it again. Business is slow, too, in the shop. When I was away in Greece the stock got run down and now I can't keep up with demand. This time of year is usually our busiest, coming up to Christmas and all that.' She stopped talking and as she listened, an incredulous look came over her face. 'You've got *trunkfuls* of clothes in the *dungeons*? Why didn't you tell me *before*?'

I could imagine his answer. 'Never occurred to me, Isabella, my dear!'

My mother was biting her lip and frowning when she replaced the receiver. Then she drummed her fingers on the table top. It seems to help her to think.

'Imagine — all that stuff just lying there! We shall have to bring it through as soon as possible. Someone will have to go over.' She looked at me.

It was not a season of the year in which she would fancy a trip to Argyll herself. At the best of times it's cold and damp in the castle but in November it would be even colder and damper, and daylight would vanish in the middle of the afternoon.

I didn't mind the idea of going — as I've said, I like to be out and about — but I didn't particularly want to go alone. And Seb plays rugby on Saturdays. Besides, going to Argyll to look at old clothes wouldn't turn him on. But it would Morag. She'd been dying to see the castle for years so I thought maybe it was time she did, before it crumbled away altogether.

My mother approved. 'That's an excellent idea. Morag's so sensible,' she added, echoing my granny, who holds up Morag and her mother as examples to my mother and me. They can bake, sew, knit, they don't go over the top ... I'll ring her mother straight away.'

Bella easily talked Morag's mother into it. She made it sound as if we were going on a visit to Balmoral. 'No, no, nothing formal is needed. They don't dress for dinner.' (We eat it in the kitchen with our plates on our laps sitting as close to the Aga cooker as we can get for warmth.) 'But I would advise some warm woollies. You know what these castles are like — great big barns of places with draughty corridors and so forth!' She gave one of her tinkly laughs, and shuddered, remembering, I expect, how the wind whistles through the gaps in the stones and the chill off the stone-flagged floors creeps up your legs. But I love it all the same.

I told Morag to bring her winter boots and the fur

lining for her anorak. She was very excited. We talked about nothing else for the next few days. Rick and John were getting fed up with us going on about it all the time. Rick said he didn't believe my grandfather really had a castle. I gave him a push and he pretended to fall over. He can be as annoying as Seb at times. It was a pity, though, that the boys couldn't have come with us, but when I suggested it to Bella she scotched the idea at once. (I didn't think she'd go for it but there'd been no harm trying.)

'Certainly not! Your grandfather is not a suitable chaperone for the four of you. You could march a pipe band through the place and he wouldn't notice.'

He's not blind or deaf or anything; he's just blissfully unaware of the outside world, as Mother says. He doesn't face up to anything until it's shoved right under his nose, which must mean that the roof was in a really bad way.

We were having a half day from school on Friday so Morag and I got on our way at lunch-time. We took a bus to Glasgow and then another one up the west coast to Oban where Grandfather was to meet us in his ancient Bentley.

'I *hope* the car will be working,' Bella said before we left, giving me a sealed envelope. 'This is for emergencies, in case it's not. You're to take a taxi if he doesn't turn up. You are *not* to hitch-hike. Or walk in the dark.'

I had no notion to do either so it wasn't a problem to make that promise.

It was dark by the time we arrived in Oban. Grandfather wasn't there when we got off the bus but I hadn't expected him to be. He'd probably only set off when the bus was due. We bought ourselves some chips and walked up and down, glad of our winter boots. But although it was cold, it was, amazingly, dry. We could smell the sea and hear the cry of the gulls over the harbour.

After half an hour, Morag asked, 'Do you think he'll come?'

'Give him time,' I said. The Bentley was usually slow to start and often had to be pushed. Grandfather might have had to go in search of someone with strong arms.

After an hour, Morag said, 'It doesn't look like he's coming, does it?'

We tracked down a taxi, and I asked how much it would cost. I counted the notes in the envelope. One short. I beat him down. We jumped in before he changed his mind.

He drove fast, as if to make up time and compensate for the loss of his pound. Morag and I held on to the side straps. On one stretch of narrow road, when we'd been travelling for about twenty minutes, we were almost blinded by the oncoming lights of another car.

'Nutcase!' roared our driver. 'Dip your lights, damn you!' He flashed his lights, and the other car flashed back, twice. And then it swept by us, narrowly missing our right bumper. I felt a slight thump where it glanced off. It was a big, old, wide car. I had recognized it all right, and the smiling face behind the wheel, even in the poor light. He'd waved as he went by. I didn't dare say to the taxi driver that that had been my grandfather's car and could he please turn round and chase after it? So I let him take us on to the castle, which sat on its rock looking like a great black fortress against the night sky. There was no moon.

We got out. Morag shivered and pulled her fur-lined hood over her head. I paid the driver.

'Are you sure this is where you want to go? I don't know that I should leave you two girls in a lonely spot like this.' There was not a light to be seen except for that made by the taxi. The caravans, which, in summer, are swarming with people, lay huddled and silent in their field. The summer visitors would all be in their snug, warm town houses.

It was fine, I assured the driver; this was where my grandfather lived.

'Well ...' He glanced over his shoulder, shrugged, then drove off. We listened to the sound of the engine dying away. Now we could hear the pounding of the North Atlantic waves against the rocks. The spray was flying high before collapsing with a soft hiss. I love to lie in bed and listen to it at night.

It was terribly dark, the kind of darkness you forget about when you live in the city. I should have thought to bring a torch. That's the kind of thing that Seb always remembers.

'Is the place haunted?' asked Morag, seizing my arm in a vice-like grip.

'I daresay it might be but they're family ghosts, and so they won't harm me. Or you,' I added, 'since you're a friend.'

Brave words! I didn't feel so brave as I led Morag up the path to the door. I had never come here without Mother and Seb, and certainly never in the pitch black. The door is massive, made of stout oak, and studded. It weighs a ton, had been built to keep fierce enemies at bay. It wouldn't budge. I pushed and pushed, but it didn't even creak.

'Grandfather must have locked it. He usually forgets.'

It was three hours before he came back. When he hadn't found us he'd presumed we weren't coming and had gone to visit a friend.

'Why didn't you phone Mother?' I demanded crossly.

'Didn't think of it, Samantha, old love. I should have, shouldn't I? Oh dear, I'm desperately sorry. You must be freezing, you poor children. So nice of you to come, though, Morag. I'm delighted to see you.' Morag couldn't speak, her teeth were chittering so much. 'Come on in now, girls. We'll go down to the kitchen and we'll have you warm in no time.'

The Aga had gone out.

'And how is Torquil?' Grandfather enquired at breakfast the next morning. We were sitting with our knees against the stove eating toasted white sliced pan, bread that my mother, who is for high fibre, calls cotton wool, and eats only when desperate. She has been known to eat it here.

'So-so,' I answered, not wanting to tell that he was homeless again and sleeping on another friend's floor until something would turn up. He is just like Mr Micawber in *David Copperfield*.

'Yes, he's taking rather a long time to settle down, that boy,' said Grandfather cheerfully. 'One of these days he'll be installed here — that'll keep him busy.'

I couldn't see my father living in the castle. Alone, listening to the wind and the rain? It was a long way to the nearest pub.

'I don't think that'll be for ages, Grandfather. You're looking great.'

'Never felt better!' His cheeks were pink and rosy and his blue eyes clear and bright. He looked in better nick than his son. The thought made me feel gloomy. What a nuisance Torquil was! For a moment I wished he could be in Marketing, like Morag's dad. She was telling Grandfather about her father's job and he was listening politely, although I knew he wouldn't have the foggiest interest in marketing anything. Though it might have been better if he had; the castle might not be in such a state.

I got up and went to look out of the back window. It was a sharp winter's day with a blue sky and pale lemony sunshine. The sea had calmed down during the night and was rippling smoothly, the peaks of each wave glistening in the sun. I'd got up before Morag and walked along the shore, turning to look from the sea back inland towards the mountains. There was snow on the tops. The whole world had looked so beautiful that I'd wanted to shout out loud. I didn't, though. Morag'd have thought I'd gone potty.

She was finding everything amazing – that was all she could say. '*Amazing!*' The thickness of the stone walls, the chill in the corridors, the view from the parapet out over the Atlantic. I'd dragged her up there when she did get up and she'd clung to me. She's not got a brilliant head for heights. Grandfather plays the bagpipes up here in summertime, I told her.

'Amazing!'

We could see the shape of islands in the distance and a small boat chugging along.

'It's cold up here, Sam. Let's go down.' As we made our way down, with her still hanging on to me, she'd said, 'What'll it be like in the dungeons?'

Perishing, we considered. We planned to go down after breakfast and to wear boots, anoraks, hats and scarves.

I rinsed our dishes under the tap – a lick and a promise, Granny calls it – and left them to drain. Grandfather was vague when I asked him if he had any drying-up cloths. I made a note to buy him some for Christmas.

'Careful of the steps, now,' he called after us, as we set off to the nether regions. He had managed to find a torch with a working battery. 'I expect they're a bit slippery. Haven't been down that way for years.'

The smell of fust struck us the moment we opened the door. I swung the torch over the steep stairs which looked as if they had been worn down by an army on the march.

'Imagine — they used to keep prisoners down here!'

Morag shivered. 'They can't have lasted long.'

'Probably not. Especially if they were done up in leg irons and manacles.'

There were still relics of those nasty things lurking about in dusty corners. Very dusty corners. We sneezed. Something scuttled across the floor. Morag screamed. I was feeling a bit nervy myself. I was thinking about Robert the Bruce in his cave with all those spiders. There could be a whole network of spiders' webs strung across the roof with dozens of the devils swinging their way from strand to strand like outward-bound adventurers. (Seb and Hari once went on a course to do that and they'd both felt giddy.) I know the Bruce thought spiders were fantastic but I'm not too turned on by them myself.

'Look!' Morag pointed. 'Those must be the trunks.'

There were six of them, great big black hulking things that would have taken half a dozen strong men to lift. We ran over to them, excited now, forgetting about spiders and things that scuttled in the dark. Morag held the torch up and I lifted the first lid.

I leant over and plunged my hands into the trunk, ready to lift out the beautiful dresses made of satin and silk, taffeta and brocade, with their trimmings of ribbons and lace. Grandfather had described some of them to us the evening before. He'd remembered the dresses his mother had worn, and his grandmother, and his wife, my grandmother, who had died before I was born. I had already decided to keep the very best of them for myself. He had said I should. They were heirlooms, after all.

The contents of the trunk were very very soft. I leaned over the high side to be able to reach further down. Morag moved around with the torch so that the light would shine directly inside the trunk.

I frowned. My hands seemed to be full of dust. I held them up, and the particles trickled from between my fingers. It looked like golden rain in the beam of the torch. We gasped. The beautiful dresses had turned to dust! The moths had got there before us.

'But we had a good weekend,' I said to Bella, 'once we got over the disappointment. The sun shone the whole time.' So the roof had been no bother. 'It was just fantastic!'

'I'm glad,' said Bella scathingly, thinking, no doubt, of how her money had gone down the drain – as far as she was concerned.

Morag and I had had a great time. We'd been outside all day long, roaming along the seashore, and after dark Grandfather had played Scrabble and Trivial Pursuits with us, and even Charades. He's a good sport, is Grandfather. And we'd made fruit punch with orange and pineapple juice and some cheap Spanish wine. And Grandfather had told us tales of his ancestors – *my* ancestors.

'What a bloodthirsty lot!' Morag had said. 'Cutting one another's throats and sticking dirks in folks' backs.'

'Only enemies, though,' Grandfather had said with a smile. 'We treat our friends differently.'

'I should have known!' said my mother, still mourning

the loss of the clothes. 'It would have been too much to expect your father's ancestors to have heard of anything sensible — like mothballs.'

8

Just Call Me Ollie

Seb

'I believe we're kin,' said the man, holding out his hand.
'Just call me Ollie!'

Bella took the hand.

'We share the same surname,' he said and laughed,
obviously pleased about that. 'Boy oh boy, is it great to
meet up with some of the other members of the clan —
the *leading* members of the clan!'

Now Bella's forebears were fishermen who fished out
of the nearby port of Newhaven while their wives sold
their wares from creels and cried 'Haddies for sale!' They
belonged to no particular clan that we know of. The man,
no doubt, was on the trail of Torquil and Grandfather.

He was an American. Well, we'd realized that even
before he opened his mouth. He had a camera round his
neck and he was wearing a plastic mac and galoshes and
a tartan tammy. It was Grandfather's clan tartan. Mine
too, of course.

I was in the shop mending a fuse. For all Bella talks
about women's lib she hasn't learned to mend a fuse yet.
When I point that out she tells me in a scathing voice
that 'it doesn't mean we all have to do the same things.'
She doesn't intend to learn how to do anything that
bores her.

'Just a second till I call Arlene,' said Ollie, and

re-opening the door, called up the steps, 'Hey, Arl, come on down! This is it!' He turned back to us. 'Your neighbour told us where to find you.'

The whole street could have told them that. We'd have a job trying to hide from anyone.

Arlene appeared in the doorway. She, too, was wearing a plastic mac, a camera and galoshes, though no tammy. Over her head she had a chiffon scarf with what looked like spangles on it. Her blue-rimmed glasses were oval-shaped.

'Isn't this just cute, Ollie! Oh, I do love old things!'

'Meet my relatives, Arl! This is – ' Ollie looked questioningly at Bella, who now spoke for the first time.

'My name is Isabella,' she announced, rising to her feet. She was wearing a green velvet cloak – it's none too warm in the shop in December with only a paraffin heater to take the chill off. 'But I'm not your relative, actually, Mr – '

He jumped in quickly. 'Ollie. Just call me – '

'Ollie. It's my husband Torquil that you want.'

'Of course! Of course! I should've known, shouldn't I, Arl?'

'But this,' went on my mother, turning to me, 'is my son Sebastian whom you *can* count as kin.'

Thanks very much, Bella! If she can dump me in it she will. Before I knew it I'd be taking them down the Royal Mile and showing them John Knox's house and Holyrood Palace.

Ollie seized my hand between both of his and pumped it up and down. Was he pleased to see me! Neither Bella nor I could get too excited. You see, we'd been through this before. Kinsmen have appeared from all over the world. We're always amazed how they track us down. On the trail of their roots, they're like terrier dogs

80

beavering for a hidden bone, and when they've got hold of it they come out with their tails wagging. This was what Ollie and Arlene were like now. They were walking round the shop exclaiming over everything. There was nothing that they didn't seem to like. Usually the relatives are astonished to find us running a second-hand clothes shop and living in a three-roomed flat.

Arlene bought three satin blouses trimmed with lace and a red velvet cloak trimmed with fur. I could see Bella warming to her. The next thing I knew she was asking them to supper that evening.

'You must meet Torquil!'

'We'd love to,' said Ollie.

I was dispatched to look for my father. I ran him to earth eventually, in a snooker hall. He was bent over the baize about to play the last black. I waited until he'd potted it. He's a brilliant snooker player. If he'd started early enough he might have made his living by it, though I doubt it. He couldn't have hacked the seriousness of it, the men playing as if their lives depended on it, hour after hour, day after day, thinking of nothing else. Torquil would always be thinking of something else.

A note changed hands between him and the man he'd been playing with. A blue note. A fiver, it looked like.

'Well, son, fancy a game?'

'OK.'

I liked playing with him. I always play better than I do with Hari. We bungle about too much. Torquil beat me, of course, but we had a good game. While we played I told him about the Americans. He said he guessed he'd better come along and do his duty. But I knew he was pleased that Bella had invited him.

He arrived on time, all spruced up, wearing his light blue corduroy suit (which had been cleaned) and carrying a bottle of wine. He must have bought that with the fiver. When Ollie and Arlene arrived they looked a bit disappointed not to see him wearing the kilt.

'I only wear it for high days and holidays, I'm afraid! Weddings, and the like.'

'What about you, Sebastian,' asked Arlene, 'don't you have kilt?'

''Course he does,' said Sam, with a smirk. 'He looks great in the kilt. He's got good knees for it – that's what Granny says!'

So then they all started going on at me. *Go on, Sebastian, put your kilt on!* In the end I had to give in, and had just come back into the living-room when the bell rang and Hari appeared with Hilary. Hari's eyes boggled at the sight of me. I'd taken good care that he'd never seen me in my kilt.

'Come in, Hari!' cried Bella, who by now had had a glass or two of wine. She'd bought a couple of bottles herself and Ollie had brought champagne. Real champagne. A magnum. 'Nice to see you, Hilary dear. Sit down, both of you, and join us – there's plenty for everyone.'

They pulled their chairs into the table. Seeing them together, I couldn't help thinking of Viola, and for a moment or two felt sort of dark and gloomy inside. I knew that if she were to walk through the door I'd feel myself lighting up and the darkness would go. Oh well! Too bad. I sat down between Hari and Ollie and put her out of my mind.

Ollie and Arlene, stripped of their plastic macs and galoshes and cameras, no longer looked like American tourists. As Bella said later, one should never judge a package by its wrapping. Ollie turned out to be a mining engineer, and was full of stories about silver and gold mines; Arlene was a historian and had done a lot of work on the Navajo Indians. They were both extremely interesting. They lived in Nevada now, though seemed to have lived in every state of the Union at some time.

'You must come and visit us, Sebastian,' said Ollie. 'Be our guest. Next summer — OK?'

'OK,' I agreed, knowing I could never raise the fare.

In the middle of the meal, the doorbell rang again. Sam had gone last time, so it was my turn. On the landing stood my grandmother. Through the open door the sound of voices and laughter and the clink of glasses and cutlery could be plainly heard. There was no disguising them. And then there was a loud pop, and a cheer. They must have opened the champagne.

'Having a party?' enquired my grandmother. Earlier on Bella had said that maybe we should go round and invite her since it was Saturday night, but with one thing and another, getting the room tidied up and so forth, we'd forgotten.

I helped Granny off with her coat. Her back was bristling with annoyance, like a cat with an annoying dog in the offing. She patted up the sides of her hair and squared her shoulders. I took her in.

Ollie had just got to his feet to make a toast.

'To Isabella, our beautiful hostess! And to Torquil, the next chief of the clan!'

'Help my goodness!' said Granny. 'All half slewed, by the looks of it!'

'Welcome, Mother-in-law!' Torquil gave her a full bow. 'Come and join our happy band!'

A glass was put into her hand, a space made for her at the table. Whatever else she had to say was drowned in the chorus of 'Isabellas' and 'Torquils'. We drank.

When we sat down again, everyone was in even more hilarious spirits.

'You always have fantastic parties, Seb,' said Hilary, as the bell rang yet again.

This time it was Rick and John and Morag looking for Sam. They were all invited in.

'Your daughter's so generous,' said Arlene to Granny. 'You'd think she was a millionaire!'

'They're wonderful people, your family, Mrs Mc-Ketterick. You're truly fortunate to have a daughter like Isabella. Just call me Arl, by the way. Could I call you by your first name? Mrs McKetterick seems so formal.'

Granny was so taken aback that she said meekly, 'Just call me Ina.' The only person who does call her Ina is Etta. And the butcher had, when he'd been around.

In no time at all Arlene had my grandmother eating out of her hand. She listened and nodded sympathetically while Granny talked about the serving of school dinners and how she had to tell the kids what was what since half the teachers nowadays weren't up to doing it. They'd gone soft since she was at school.

'That was a very long time ago, mind!'

'I can't believe that, Ina.'

Ina almost blushed.

At the end of the evening, when I was walking her home, she said, 'She was an awful nice woman, that Arlene.'

On the way back I passed a crowd of girls who are in the year above me at school. They're a crowd I could do without seeing; they're good at lounging against walls and calling out remarks.

'Hey, look, there's Sebbie!' shouted one of them. 'Looks more like Debbie!'

I'd forgotten about my kilt. I glanced down at my

knees. They were now doing their killing-themselves-laughing bit. So what! There was nothing wrong with wearing the kilt. Any real Scotsman would be prepared to wear one. Many do. As I walked back down the street I kept my head up and felt the kilt swirling round my knees. I felt a bit like a clan chieftain going to meet the enemy. I was in the mood for it. If I'd had a dirk in my hand I'd have turned and charged them with a blood-curdling yell. I'd have liked to have seen them scuttling away up the street — in terror.

Ollie and Arlene hired a car and went on their pilgrimage to Argyll. Grandfather had been warned and was up on the parapet playing the bagpipes when they arrived. They stayed with him at the castle; he insisted. He loves company, as long as he doesn't have to produce food. Sliced bread and tea's his limit. Arlene did the cooking and made marvellous stew and roasted sides of beef and legs of lamb. He told us about the meals over the phone, making them sound like mediaeval banquets.

'We've missed ourselves there,' said Granny. 'We should all have gone. I could go a good leg of lamb right now.' (We were having lentil roast with red cabbage for supper.)

I said I wasn't sure about eating lamb. 'Some of it's still contaminated since Chernobyl, even after all this time. Like venison is.'

'Oh, you and your horror stories!'

The other thing that Grandfather rang up to tell us was that he had solved his roof problem. I had taken the call.

'How do you mean — *solved* it? Where did you get the money from?'

'Ollie.'

'Ollie?'

'Yes, our American cousin. Very generous man. He wanted to do something for the castle, he said, being kin and all that. The ties of blood are strong, Sebastian — never forget that!'

'But how can he afford it?'

'He's a millionaire! Imagine — a millionaire in the family!'

He wasn't exactly in the family, I pointed out, being but distantly related. Grandfather made it sound as if we'd hit the jackpot. It seemed that Ollie, as well as being a mining engineer, owned a number of mines. That was how he'd made his millions, or had started making them; then he'd set up an investment company, and had bought real estate in California and Nevada. 'He's obviously got his head screwed on,' said Grandfather.

Our family, instead of buying real estate, had been selling it bit by bit, to help pay taxes, until there was only a narrow strip left round the castle rock. We could have used Ollie's advice — and money — years ago.

He hadn't put up the money for a whole new roof — that would cost hundreds of thousands — but he had put enough to cover the immediate repair. Even that was a few thousands. Scaffolding alone would cost a thousand or two.

'That's fantastic of him,' I said. None of the previous visiting kin had seen fit to contribute ten p to the castle upkeep. And when I came to think about it, I saw no reason why they should. But it *was* good of Ollie.

When Ollie and Arlene returned from Argyll, we were all there to greet them, our grandmother as well. She couldn't get over knowing a millionaire. Torquil kissed

Arlene's hand and expressed his 'undying gratitude' to Ollie. My father doesn't half know how to turn it on. Ollie said they'd been only too pleased to be of help. Arlene smile behind her blue-rimmed glasses.

'And now,' said Ollie, 'put on your glad rags! We're going out to celebrate. This is our last night in Scotland so we want to make it one to remember.'

Bella and Sam went diving down to the shop to rummage amongst the stock to find something to wear. Granny went home to put on her best black polyester dress with a diamante clip at the neck. You were always smart if you wore black, she claimed. Torquil unearthed an ancient dinner suit from a trunk and stuck a chrysanthemum in the buttonhole. He said he used to wear the suit when he went to dinner dances with my mother. Arlene insisted I put on my kilt. She herself was wearing a long peacock-blue taffeta dress and Ollie had on black trousers and a jacket and bow tie in our clan tartan.

' "Putting on the glad rags",' sang Torquil, while we waited for Bella and Sam to come back. ' "Putting on the top hat ... " ' And he spun around and twirled an imaginary stick as if he was Fred Astaire.

Ollie and Arlene took us to a very expensive restaurant, the kind we could never go to if we saved for twenty years. The waiters were so polite and well-trained that they didn't even let themselves blink at the long peach satin gloves which Bella was wearing to match her dress or the peach-coloured feathers trailing from her hair. She had a Ginger Rogers' look about her. Sam had on a skinny burnt-orange coloured dress with fringes round the bottom and a band round her head.

'Twenties style,' she informed me.

She looked a bit odd – like a cross between a North American Indian and a lampshade – but I thought I'd better not say so. Everyone was in great spirits.

'It's simply marvellous to know the castle has had a reprieve,' said Torquil.

He was right — it *was* marvellous, but the roof would only be patched, not fixed. The family is good at patching and forgetting. *Each Day As It Comes*: that should be our motto. Instead of: *Valour Will Out*. I knew, though, that at some point we would have to think seriously about what to do with the castle. It couldn't just stand there for ever without any money being spent on its upkeep. It *wouldn't* stand. We wouldn't think about that tonight, however.

'I must say,' said Bella, smoothing the long gloves up her arms, 'it is rather nice to put on one's glad rags once in a while.'

9

Ding Dong Merrily on High

Sam

Torquil got a Christmas job playing Santa Claus. I wouldn't have thought he was ideal for it – his face is too thin and not at all rosy and he doesn't look old enough. Make-up would soon sort that out, he said, and a white wig and beard. He was pleased with himself and went round humming 'Jingle Bells'. He likes acting, and telling stories to small children. And he likes to be able to tell my mother (and grandmother) that he's working.

Morag and I went to see him in the store. The loudspeakers were spewing out Christmas music. 'Ding dong merrily on high, in heaven the bells are ringing ...' It was Saturday afternoon, and murder in the toy department, what with the heat, and kids pushing, and mums yelling and trying to yank the kids back, and babies squalling. Most of the mums looked as if they'd much rather be at home with their feet up drinking tea. Even Morag, who's bananas about small kids (unlike me), didn't look too thrilled at the sight of them. She'd like to have half a dozen children of her own one day, which is even more unlike me. Well, how could I ever become a great artist if I had half a dozen Flowers hanging on to my easel?

Through the mob we could just make out Santa sitting in the doorway of his grotto flanked by seven plaster of

Paris dwarfs. A sea of kids' heads bobbed round him. He didn't have time to notice us.

We hung around for a while in case he had a quiet spell. The tills were ringing merrily. Mothers and fathers and grannies and grandpas were queuing up to pay for machine guns and Action Force Mobile Command Centres and Everything You Need for Solar Invasion. *Kill, kill, kill!* It was just as well Bella wasn't there; she'd have exploded. I could just hear her. *Peace on earth, good will to men!* She seldom goes into big stores, especially at Christmas; she can't stand the sight of people flinging their money about as if it grew on bushes. She says it's obscene when other people in the world are starving.

Morag and I left without seeing Santa; we got fed up being dunted in the stomach with metre-wide boxed shopping centres and hamburger stalls. When we did see Torquil later, he looked like a wrung-out dish rag.

'Never mind,' said Morag, ever sensible, 'there's only one Saturday in every week.'

He brightened. 'How right you are, Morag!' he declared, and disappeared into the pub on the corner.

The street was beginning to look Christmassy. Most shops had a few coloured lights in their windows, some had small trees, and even Mr Murchie had draped a couple of strands of gold tinsel over a china ewer and basin. They were the only things that he had in the window, apart from his fat tiger cat who likes to sit with his nose pressed against the dusty glass watching the outside world. When he sees the Quinn's cat coming, his eyes widen and he tries to leap through the window. He's a dumb cat. Sometimes he lies on car roofs and once, in the dark, Mr Quinn drove off with him on top. Tiger had to leap off at the corner, which nearly caused

Mr Quinn to have a heart attack and crash into a lamp-post.

My mother was preoccupied with finding new stock for the shop. As soon as she got the dress rack filled up, it emptied again. This was her best time of year for selling. It was party time.

She decided to advertise.

I was so busy reading her ad in the *Edinburgh Evening News* — 'Interesting clothes wanted, '20s, '30s, '40s, or earlier ...' that I didn't see Viola coming towards me until she was almost walking up my legs.

'Hello, Sam.'

'Oh, hi, Viola! How are you?'

Then I saw she wasn't alone. She had a boy with her. He was wearing a blazer, with a whole row of fountain pens sticking out of the top pocket — real fountain pens, not biros. She introduced us. His name was Julian. We nodded at one another. Viola and I chatted for a minute or two about nothing very much while Julian stood a little to one side looking bored. He had the kind of face that easily looks bored.

'I'd better get on with my round,' I said. 'Have a good Christmas, Viola!'

'You, too, Sam.' She hesitated. 'Maybe I'll see you over the holidays?'

'Maybe. I'll still be on my round.'

As I said cheerio and moved off, I heard Julian ask, 'Who was *that*?'

That scruff, I suppose he meant, in an old anorak and trousers with a newspaper sack over her shoulder. I went home feeling all bristly and annoyed.

'I met Viola,' I told Seb.

'Oh?' He made it sound as if he wasn't interested.

'She's got a new boyfriend. He's called Julian and he

wears a blazer stuffed with fountain pens.' I knew I would hurt Seb if I said that, and yet I had to say it – it was part of feeling irritated at the way that twit Julian had looked at me. As if I smelled bad.

Seb shrugged and turned away and didn't speak to me for the rest of the evening. But I didn't see why I should say sorry to him. Well, it wasn't my fault that Viola had got herself a new boyfriend, was it? (Or had she? She might just have been walking up the street with him. I put that thought out of my mind.)

We'd hardly started to eat when the phone began to ring. It seemed as if half the old ladies in Edinburgh had interesting clothes to sell. Bella tried to sort out the pure fabrics from the polyesters over the phone and wrote down the most likely addresses.

'We'll make a start tomorrow, Samantha.'

I was happy to go with her. It was a chance to get out and about and see inside other people's houses. So, OK, I'm nosy!

The first lady lived beside the zoo. She said you could hear the lions roaring at night. She liked hearing them. Otherwise it could be very quiet once she turned off the television. She was a widow.

Her bungalow was stiflingly hot, and very neat and tidy. When I rumpled the rug, she got up to straighten it.

'Sorry,' I mumbled, and tried not to lean back against the cushions.

She had no clothes of any interest to us, we could see that from the start – she took a pride in always having worn good tweeds and twin sets – but we had to stay and drink tea and eat Rich Tea biscuits and listen to her telling us how horrible the neighbours were. They drove up and down the street in their expensive cars and didn't even give you the time of day.

'You could lie at the back of the door for three days and no one would even care.'

'Lonely people are always lonelier at Christmas,' said Bella, as we walked down the street afterwards. It was dead quiet, all the curtains were drawn, and nothing was moving. I thought of the taxis weaving in and out of the parked cars in our street and the people going in and out of the restaurants and pubs. But then the widow wouldn't like that, either. She'd complain about the noise. Each to her own, as my granny would say.

The next woman lived in a huge, cold, Victorian detached house surrounded by a walled garden. It smelt musty as we went in. The old lady, whose name was Mrs Mellon, seemed to be living in one room at the back, heated (or rather, not heated) by a one-bar electric fire, and filled with old cartons and boxes and empty tins. I wouldn't need to worry about rumpling the rug here. Two scraggy cats were sitting so close to the fire that it was a wonder they weren't scorching their coats. I turned up the collar of my jacket and kept my hands in my pockets. It's not always comfortable running a second-hand clothes business. But it's interesting. I was thinking I'd like to paint Mrs Mellon and her cats.

She was wearing a mangy fur coat and sheepskin-lined boots with broken zips. She had a sweet face and bright eyes.

'Sit down, please do sit down.' She fussed over us. 'Now what can I offer you in the way of refreshment?'

'Nothing, thank you very much, Mrs Mellon,' said Bella, 'though it's kind of you to offer. But we've just eaten.'

Mrs Mellon sat down herself. She wanted to know

all about us. Where did we live, how many in the family? She seemed to find everything fascinating. 'Your grandmother works in your school serving dinners? How brave of her!' I could imagine Granny humphing at that.

'It's so nice to have company!' sighed Mrs Mellon. She'd probably not spoken to anyone all day. I was beginning to feel like a social worker. I wondered if she'd remembered why we'd come.

She did have some clothes, however: masses of them, in old trunks. They smelt as if they'd been shut up for a hundred years, but they didn't fall apart in our hands.

To begin with, she didn't want to take any payment.

'I must pay you something,' Bella insisted.

'But I don't really want any money. I've got more than I need.'

My mother glanced at the one-bar electric fire, then decided to speak bluntly. I saw the look come into her eye.

'Mrs Mellon, why don't you spend some of your money on heating the house? And have you had enough to eat today? When did you last have a proper meal?'

Not for a long time, as far as we could gather. Mrs Mellon seemed to live on crackers and blue cheese and cups of tea and to think it would be wickedly extravagant to spend too much money on food and heat. And she was worried that her money would run out before she died. That was the crux of the matter, as my mother said later. Bella expounded on the advantages of sheltered housing, though I didn't think she'd convince Mrs Mellon, who had spent the last fifty years in this house. My feet were beginning to feel as if they'd been in the freezer.

It was ten o'clock before we got away.

'I've enjoyed your visit so much,' said Mrs Mellon

wistfully, when she escorted us to the door.

I looked out into the night. The garden was full of black shadows and the wind was rustling the branches of the trees. I shivered.

'Mrs Mellon,' said my mother, turning back to her, 'why don't you come and spend Christmas Day with us?'

'Well, one more won't make any difference,' said Bella, as we rode home on the warm bus.

Apart from ourselves – and Granny, of course, and Torquil, and Grandfather, who was coming from Argyll – we were having Mr Murchie, who has no family, and the Quinns, who have no children, and Bella's friend Maudie, who always spends Christmas with us, and Granny's friend Etta, who always spends Christmas with Granny and, therefore, with us.

'That's twelve, counting Mrs Mellon,' I said.

'We can manage that at the table, with both leaves out. Mrs Mellon's tiny, after all. There's not much of her – poor old soul.'

At that point we hadn't known about the forthcoming Orkney invasion.

When we arrived home (starving, and carrying brown-paper parcels of fish and chips), Seb said, 'Clementina rang. They're coming to Edinburgh for Christmas. It's all right, though, don't get worked up! – they're not planning to stay here, they're going to Donald's sister, but they want to come for Christmas Day.'

The Flowers hit Edinburgh three days before Christmas and were carted off straight away by their father to see Santa. I went with them.

We had to take our turn in the queue. Santa was

lifting each child on to his knee and speaking to him
before he handed over the parcels.

'I want a doll's house from Santa,' said Daisy. (I knew
that Donald had made her one and Clementina had made
furniture and curtains and knitted little rugs.)

'I want a dolly that says mummy and does wee-wees,'
said Buttercup. (She was getting a cloth doll that didn't
do either.)

'I want a wee-wee doll, too,' cried Clover. (Donald
had made her a farm. He and Clementina do not shop
in toy departments.)

'You'll have to take what Santa gives you,' said
Donald firmly.

Daisy and Buttercup were getting more and more
excited as we shuffled up the queue. They wriggled and
jiggled and wouldn't stand still. Clover stuck her thumb
in her mouth and kept her eyes glued on Santa.

Finally it was our turn.

'Well, well!' said Santa. 'Three lovely little girls! And
what are *your* names?'

'Daisy!'

'Buttercup!'

'Clover!'

'Three beautiful flowers,' said Santa, holding out his
hand first to Clover.

She was not shy. (You must be joking!) She slid on
to his red knee, still keeping her thumb in her mouth
and her eyes fixed on his face.

'And what would *you* like from Santa, Clover?'

'S'not Santa!' she cried, pulling her thumb from her
mouth and yanking off his beard. 'S'Uncle Torquil!'

'Uncle Torquil!' shrieked the other two Flowers and
fell on him.

The rest of the queue collapsed like a row of skittles

going down. The crying of small children filled the toy department for the next half-hour.

Torquil was relieved when his stint as Santa came to an end. He said it had had its trying moments, not least when Clover gave the show away. He'd almost been sacked, but the store manager, while dancing with rage, had realized that it wouldn't be easy to find a new Santa at such a late date.

Torquil arrived on Christmas Day in a very good mood, bringing presents for everyone. He gave Seb and me new watches, good ones, not Mickey Mouse affairs.

'He'll have spent every penny he's earned, you can bet your boots on that!' said Granny. But she was pleased enough to get the silk scarf he gave her.

The Flowers were up to 'high doh', as Granny put it. She elected not to be seated near them at the table, having had enough things spilt in her lap by them in the past. The table was actually two tables put together — one borrowed from Mr Murchie, who'd also lent some chairs. As had Maudie. Mrs Quinn had lent plates and glasses. And she'd baked the mince pies and shortbread. Maudie had made the Christmas cake. Everyone had brought bottles of wine and flowers. Seb and I had spent hours and hours peeling potatoes and parsnips.

He'd had a Christmas card from Viola. I saw it on the shelf beside his bed, but I didn't say anything or ask if he'd sent her one. He'd have told me to mind my own business if I had.

Grandfather, too, was in excellent form, having driven over from Argyll in the old Bentley the day before and broken down only once. He'd been towed fifty miles to the nearest garage by the AA, which had pleased him, as it had saved on petrol.

Then Mrs Mellon arrived in a taxi filled with boxes and boxes of candied fruits and dates and chocolates.

'I decided you were right, Isabella — it was time I started to spend some money. I might as well enjoy it while I can.'

Isabella was wearing a long emerald green gown, with an orchid (brought by Torquil) pinned to her hair. She was so much up in the air that she looked as if she might begin to fly at any moment, which would mean that Seb and I would have to organize the dinner completely. I was trying to work out when to put the brussel sprouts on.

There were now seventeen of us gathered together drinking pre-dinner fizzy wine and pulling crackers. Clover was sitting on my back like a monkey. Then the bell rang again. I only just heard it over the din everybody was making.

I looked out of the window. There was a taxi standing in the street. As I watched, I saw the driver open the back door and help out an old lady.

'Who's this coming, Mother?' I asked.

'Oh, it looks like one of the old ladies that I bought clothes from up on the Braid Hills. I'd forgotten I'd invited her. Go and open the door, Samantha, there's a dear!'

In the course of the next hour three more elderly ladies arrived in taxis from different parts of the city.

Granny was 'beside herself', as she herself might have put it.

'What on earth do you think you're doing, Isabel?' she demanded, following her daughter into the kitchen. 'I know it's Christmas and all that, but there *is* a limit! You'd think you were a millionaire.'

'For today,' said Isabella, turning to her mother with a smile, 'I feel like a millionaire.'

10

A Good New Year

Seb

New Year's a funny time. Everyone gets excited and thinks that they're going to have a fantastic time. They seem to imagine that something special will happen. Nearly always they're disappointed.

Bella doesn't get excited. She hates New Year. You might have thought she'd have the biggest and noisiest party in the street, but not so. She goes to bed before it comes in. She puts out the lights, and first-footers can ring and ring, but they won't get her up. Before she goes to bed, though, the whole place is turned upside down for its special Hogmanay-cleaning, the only time in the year when it does get properly cleaned and tidied up. This is one of our grandmother's traditions that our mother carries on.

'No good Scotswoman would let the New Year come into a dirty house,' says Granny, who cleans her own flat from top to bottom. 'It would mean bad luck for a twelvemonth.' That thought seems to please her.

Our cleaning took all day and lasted well into the evening. Sam and I had to do our own bedrooms. We filled five black plastic bags with rubbish. Bella, wearing yellow rubber gloves and a turban on her head, set to and scoured the kitchen; Sam vacuumed and dusted the hall and the sitting-room; and I got the windows to clean. I felt like a professional window cleaner as I stood balancing on the outside sill. Sam had to stop vacuuming to hold on to my legs. She tried on a bit of blackmail while she was at it.

'Will you lend me your new tranny, Seb? Just for tomorrow afternoon.'

'You're joking!' I sloshed the wet shammy across the window and watched the excess water run down the wall. I didn't think I'd get on very well earning my living as a window cleaner.

'I'll let you go if you don't!'

'Go on then!' I looked two storeys down into the basement area, where old Mrs Mooney had just pegged out a line of dishcloths. They sagged limply in the damp air. I'd be pretty limp myself if I were to hit the ground down there. 'What's keeping you?'

'Mother would give me a row if I let you fall. And it'd be an awful mess for Mrs Mooney to clean up.'

I was quite glad to come in and do the insides of the windows. Hari arrived, and I threw him a shammy. I told him it would be good for him to see how the other half of the male population has to suffer. His mother would never let him or his father so much as touch a duster, in spite of the fact that she works full-time as a nurse and has to come home after a day on the ward and start cooking and cleaning. Lucky Hari! I say, which can guarantee to get a rise out of Bella and Sam. My mother once tried to have a 'little chat' with Hari's mother and tell her the world had changed and all that, and how ridiculous it was for Mrs Patel to run herself into the ground, but she got nowhere. Mrs Patel just smiled and nodded and said that she was too old to change her ways. Women's work was women's work, as far as she was concerned, and that was that. But Hari, when he goes to Hilary's for supper, dries the dishes while she washes. He dries each one very carefully, taking his time, not slinging them half wet into the cupboard, the way I do.

Hari obligingly took on some of our windows, making a better job of them than I was doing. He declined, however, Sam's invitation to have a go with the vacuum cleaner. She loathes vacuuming, says the whining sound it makes travels right up through her body into her head and gives her electric shocks. She tugs the machine behind her as if it were a vicious animal. She snarls at it, and it snarls back. When Rick came round she gave him the hall to do, and he ran up and down using the vacuum like a charger. He took a few nicks out of the skirting boards.

In the kitchen, Bella was swearing. We knew she must be on to the cooker.

'Do you kids *ever* clean up after you boil milk over?' she was yelling.

Our next caller was Torquil, but when he saw what we were up to he beat a fast retreat. He also finds the sound of the vacuum cleaner disturbing. But he stayed long enough to tell us that he had got a job as a film extra for January. Not marvellous money, of course, but it was something, and he likes being around in the film and television world.

At noon, our grandmother arrived for half-time inspection.

'It's good to see you all working for a change!'

At nine o'clock in the evening, we were allowed to hang up our dusters and cloths at last.

'I'm not doing another thing!' Sam declared.

I went for an Indian carry-out, and we ate, the three of us sitting slumped round the table, exhausted. It seemed a crazy way to end a year.

'What's the point?' Sam demanded. 'It'll all be dusty again tomorrow.'

'But at least I know it's clean now,' Bella retorted and then went to lie in the bath for an hour so that she, too, would enter the new year unsullied.

Sam got up and washed the dishes without any arguing. She was going to a party with Morag and Rick and John. She was being allowed to go on the understanding that she would return home with Morag to her house afterwards, that they would be escorted by the boys, and that she wouldn't touch alcohol, and certainly not drugs! At home she's allowed the odd glass of wine, but not when she's out. (I couldn't tell you if she sticks to the rule or not!)

Bella emerged from the bathroom in a flaming orange kimono with green dragons rampaging up her back, her wet hair swathed in a towel, to wring a final promise from Sam.

'Brownie's honour.' Sam raised two fingers in salute. (She'd only lasted three weeks in the Brownies, when she was seven. She hadn't liked pretending she was an elf.) 'Anyway, Mother, you've got quite the wrong idea about this party. There'll be *no* drugs. It'll just be a quiet affair, and Jill's parents are *not* going out.'

'I know all about Hogmanay parties,' said Bella grimly. It was all right for her to have had her wild flings in her youth, but she was going to do her best to stop us following her example. 'People get drunk *and* stupid.' She shuddered.

Sam departed wearing a bright blue taffeta dress with what she informed me were 'puffed' shoulders. She looked all puffed out herself in the dress. It had come from the shop, of course.

'And what about you, Sebastian?' Bella asked. 'What are you going to do?'

I shrugged. I wasn't sure. I wasn't too bothered about doing anything very much.

'I might go out with Hari and Hilary.'

They called in about eleven. They were going to a party. I knew the girl who was giving it. She's called Olive, and I'd gone out with her a couple of times, a while back, before I started going with Viola.

'Are you coming with us then?' asked Hari.

'Come on, Seb!' said Hilary. 'You can't sit in the house on your own on Old Year's night.'

OK, I agreed, I'd go with them, though I might not stay for long.

There were about thirty at the party when we arrived, and two or three were already on their way to getting drunk. A couple of girls were dancing to a record; everyone else was hanging around. The television, which couldn't be heard over the sound of the music, was on in the corner. A comedian in a kilt was opening and shutting his mouth and every few seconds he creased himself laughing at his own jokes. Then on came the Scottish country dancers. I could feel the heaviness of New Year weighing on the scene. No doubt Sam was having a good time, and my grandmother always enjoys Hogmanay. She was going to Etta's this year. She and her cronies have their own ritual; they take it turnabout to go to one another's houses and have the traditional things to eat like shortbread and black bun and whisky and port to drink. They watch the telly until midnight and sing along with the performers. And when twelve strikes, they get up to join hands and sing 'Auld Lang Syne'. Granny says New Year means more to her than Christmas.

Another crowd arrived at Olive's party, one that we didn't know. Gatecrashers. But once they were in, they were in. Some of them were so drunk they were staggering and one threw up in the hall before he got to the bathroom. There was no sign of Olive's parents. They'd gone to visit her aunt, she said. She wasn't looking too happy. Well, who would be when she had to clean up someone else's vomit? No one else would do it, and the boy who'd made the mess had locked himself in the bathroom. There was a queue now outside the door, and someone was banging on it shouting, 'Get out of there, I'm desperate!'

'Have some black bun,' said Olive, passing round the plate. She kept passing things round. I felt sorry for her. She was nervous, couldn't relax.

I said I'd already eaten. The curry was lying uneasily in my stomach. I leant against the wall. It was ten to twelve. I was conscious of each minute ticking by. Last chance to do anything this year. I wished I were walking on top of Arthur's Seat and looking down on the city from above; it would be cool up there, and quiet.

Two minutes to go. Then one. The music was killed, and the television sound turned up. We heard the first stroke of Big Ben chiming the hour. The first stroke of a brand-new year. And even I, in my sourish mood, felt a little upsurge of excitement. Anything could happen in this year. It was a new start, after all.

We cheered and shouted 'Happy New Year' and went round the room, the boys kissing the girls, the girls kissing one another, and the boys slapping each other on the back.

The first-foot, who had been planted outside the door before midnight, rang the bell and was admitted. It was Hari. It has to be a dark man. Hari had offered. 'I'm the darkest here,' he'd said, with a little smile. He was carrying a lump of coal, which he presented to Olive with a bow. I wished it was easy as that to be brought good luck.

Now that I'd seen the New Year in, I wanted to be away. I said goodbye to Olive, who was too distracted by someone smashing glasses to notice me going, and to Hari and Hilary, who were dancing cheek to cheek.

It was a fine frosty evening with a rash of stars across the sky. The air smelt good after the fug of the party.

The streets were full of people singing, dancing, shouting, straggling across the road. Some were drunk; some just happy. I wandered down towards the bridge and leaned over the parapet to look down into the dark, quiet-flowing Water of Leith.

Then I turned and leaned my back against the stone and saw a girl coming running down the road, her dark hair flying out behind her. The way she moved was familiar. I straightened up.

She had to stop at the traffic light. She waited, leaning forward on her toes as if she'd had to brake suddenly and was anxious to get on her way. The light changed to red, and the green man lit up. She stepped out again, with a long stride. She hadn't seen me.

She crossed the road. She drew level with me.

'Viola!'

She stopped abruptly, and turned towards me.

'*Sebastian!*'

'Happy New Year!' I took her hands and kissed her before I had time to think about it.

'Happy New Year!' She laughed, tossing back her head, flicking her hair away from her face.

'Where are you going?' I asked.

'I was at a party and I was *hating* it – everyone was

getting drunk – so I decided to go home.'

'Me too.'

'It's nice to see you.'

'You too.'

'Thank you for your Christmas card.'

'Thank you for yours.'

We had to move in towards the bridge to let a crowd surge past. They shouted 'Happy New Year' to us and we shouted it back. I thought again of the peace and quiet there would be on top of Arthur's Seat and wished that I could take Viola up there.

What was I thinking! That I wanted to start going out with her again? To have her as my girlfriend? We could, of course, go out from time to time without having to go steady with all the bother that seems to bring in its wake. Emotional ups and downs, Bella calls them. Part of life, she says. I can do without them, myself. Sam says I run away from emotional things – like most males.

I realized that while I was thinking my thoughts Viola was standing there watching me, waiting for me to say something. I wasn't quite sure what to say. She spoke.

'Can we be friends again?'

'I'd like to.'

'So would I.'

Friends: that was what we would be. Just good friends. This time I was going to play it cool and not even bother about her parents or what they thought of me. In fact, neither of us needed to go anywhere near the other's family. Families just complicate matters. Especially families like hers and mine. Both of them, each in their very different ways, are minefields, and I didn't see why Viola and I should have to pick our way across them.

I asked if I could take her home. I could hardly let her

wander the street alone on a night like this.

'Thanks, Sebastian. I don't like being out on my own at New Year with so many drunks about. I promised Mother I'd come home with Cynthia, but she didn't want to leave the party, and I didn't want to wait for her.'

I took Viola's hand — a purely friendly gesture — and we crossed the road. As we reached the opposite kerb, I saw two women coming along the pavement walking jauntily. They were both squarish-shaped and they had their arms linked. One of them looked terribly familiar. I debated whether I could drag Viola back across the road, but I wasn't quick enough.

'Seb!' cried my grandmother. 'Is that you, son? Have you got a New Year kiss for your granny, then?'

She put out her arms and grasped me to her bosom. I could smell the port on her breath.

'You mind Mrs Robins, don't you, Seb? We're just on our way home from Etta's. We had a lovely evening, so we did.'

I then had to wish Mrs Robins a good New Year and kiss her, which gave Granny the chance to see whom I was with.

'It's Viola, isn't it? I thought it was! A Happy New Year to you, dear.' She gave Viola a hearty kiss on the cheek and took hold of her hands. 'Well, well, isn't this nice?' She pumped Viola's hands up and down keeping time to her words. 'He's been missing you, hen.'

Then my dear grandmother turned to me and winked. 'So you've got your wee sweetheart back again, eh, Seb? You'll be a happy lad the night!'

11

A Sore Trial

Sam

January was one of those months that you wouldn't want to have a second time round. To start with, Granny didn't get away to Morocco as Etta had flu. That didn't put her in the best of moods!

'Etta's aye been inclined to illness. She's got a weak chest.' As my mother said, Granny made it sound as if it was a failing on Etta's part rather than a misfortune.

Then we had a plague of mice in our flat. They seemed to spend the night dancing the Highland Fling in the kitchen. Their footprints were everywhere, in the frying pan, on bars of soap, and they even knocked the top off the butter dish and traipsed over that. My mother read us lectures about not leaving food out or dropping crumbs. But the flat couldn't have been cleaner, after all the redding up it had had for New Year. We borrowed the Quinn's cat and next morning there were five corpses laid out on the kitchen floor for us to admire, but once the cat went home the mice were out and at it again.

'These old flats are impossible,' said Bella, after a mouse had hiked across her bed when she was in it. They were getting dead cheeky. 'Makes me think a modern bungalow might not be so bad.'

'You know you'd hate it,' said Seb. 'Apart from the fact that you couldn't afford it.'

I suggested we got a cat for our own but Bella wouldn't go for it; she said she'd enough on her plate supporting the three of us, and where could we keep its litter tray? And who would clean the litter tray? She didn't get any answers to that one.

We called in the Council, who sent along their vermin exterminator. The place smelt for a while but at least we got peace at night. I thought of the Great Plague in London when the city had been overrun with rats, and shivered.

We'd only just sorted that out when we went down with flu, the three of us at the same time. It was a particularly virulent strain, so everybody said, and the only thing to do was to lie down under it. We had to close the shop, not that there's much going at that time of year, anyway. People have spent all their money at Christmas and the New Year sales.

Granny looked after us. She filled our hot-water bottles, brought us hot drinks, doled out aspirins. She seemed to be enjoying having us flat on our backs, too weak to talk back. For once she and Mother didn't argue.

'Trust you all to get ill at once! You're a sore trial, and that's a fact.'

She marched up and down like a matron on a hospital ward and brought us news from the outside world. She'd met Viola. 'Nice lass, that. You've got good taste, Seb, I will say that for you.' Viola had sent us her best wishes for a speedy recovery. Morag was asking for me, Mr Murchie was asking for our mother, and the Quinns wanted to know if they could do anything. Torquil was away filming in the Western Isles. He'd sent us a postcard of the sun setting over the Atlantic.

'Filming!' snorted Granny. 'Idling around, if you ask me.'

After the first couple of days when I had felt really rotten, I found I was quite enjoying myself. It was warm and cosy in bed and I'd lots to read. I'd been to the library the day before I fell ill and had got out half a dozen books. So apart from wanting to see everybody, I didn't feel like hurrying back to school. Rain was scudding against the window and every now and then a gust of wind rattled the frame.

Morag was allowed to come in for an hour or so in the afternoon and made to sit well away from me.

'You're not wanting the flu now, are you, Morag?'

'What about you, Mrs McKetterick? Aren't you worried you'll catch it?'

'Flu? Not me! I don't get things like that. I haven't had flu in years.'

I was sure that the influenza germs wouldn't dare attack my granny. And I must say that she looked the picture of health. Our illness seemed to have given her an extra burst of energy and brought roses to her cheeks – to use one of her own sayings.

Our days of idleness passed. We got back on to our feet, Seb returned to school, and I realized that I'd soon have to follow suit.

The day I went back, Granny took to her bed. I was sent round to play nurse. It was nothing, she said; she'd soon be back on her feet again. She had me running up and down like a skivvy. The hot-water bottle was too hot and then too cold, she wanted the gas fire turned up and then down, she wanted a hot drink and then a cold one.

'Did you hear me, Sam? I'm needing some water.'

I hadn't heard her. I'd been standing at the window looking down into the street, thinking. About Rick. He'd been kind of funny to me that day, sort of off-hand, as if he hadn't been all that pleased to see me. I'd been looking forward to seeing him after being away from school for a week. He'd sent me a card and rung up once but he hadn't come round. I'd thought his mother probably hadn't wanted him to catch flu from us. She's a bit of a fusspot.

'Water,' groaned Granny. Her voice was not as strong as it usually was, which was not surprising.

I fetched the water and held the cup while she drank. Going near her was like closing in on a fiery furnace. She seemed to have a terrific temperature on her. We'd all had when we were at our worst.

'Maybe I should call the doctor, Granny.'

'Doctor! I'm wanting no doctor. What can he do?'

Nothing much, I knew. It was just a case of lying low and keeping warm until the worst passed. But I could see that Granny was not going to be an easy patient. She doesn't like being helpless and at other people's mercy.

When she dozed off for a bit, I went round to Morag's. She was watching *Neighbours*.

'Morag, I want to ask you something.'

'Shush up, Sam! I'm listening.' She was frowning at the screen.

'What's going on with Rick?'

She didn't answer.

I got between her and the television set. 'Tell me!'

'What do you want me to tell you?'

'Is he seeing someone else?'

'Oh, OK! Yes, he is.'

I punched the off-button and killed *Neighbours*. I told Morag to tell me everything.

It turned out that Rick had started going out with Mandy, another girl in our year at school, not a friend of ours, someone I only knew by sight. He'd started seeing her when I was off ill. She's got long black hair and comes to school wearing so much mascara that it's a wonder she can open her eyes, and she thinks she can twist boys round her little finger.

'She made a real play for him.'

'You might have told me!'

'I didn't want to upset you when you were ill. Besides, I thought he might ditch her when you came back.'

I called Rick and Mandy a few names until Morag told me to calm down and not to let her mother hear me.

'They can both go jump in the river!' I declared. 'And I hope they drown.'

'The Water of Leith's not very deep,' said Morag, which made me giggle, and then want to cry. But I wasn't going to cry over Rick Watson! He was a jerk, and not worth getting steamed up over. We'd had some good times together, the four of us, and now he'd had to go and spoil it. Morag was still friendly with John but she said it wasn't the same. She didn't like it as much, being on her own with him. They didn't seem to have a lot to talk about. It was going round in a foursome that had been so good. Why is it that nothing can ever stand still, even for just a little while?

I sighed. 'I'd better go back and see to Granny.'

She had woken up and was in a right bad mood. *Get me this, get me that, what are you doing, get a move on, faster, faster!* My own legs were still feeling weak. I'd known I should have stayed in my bed! Bella had got me started on *Wuthering Heights*. I could have done to snuggle down with that and shut out everything else.

I had to sleep over at Granny's, on the too-short bed-settee. I'm not that tall but either my feet dangled over the end or I got my neck all scrunched up and woke with the right side of it stiff.

'I'm not feeling well enough to sleep on that thing,' I complained to my mother.

'We can't leave your grandmother on her own overnight.' My mother was obviously not going to offer to sleep on the settee herself. She's three or four inches taller than me.

'Old people are in a special risk category with flu,' said Seb, not sounding in the least bit concerned. He was being so cheerful these days (because of Viola) that he was getting on my nerves.

'Gran's not that old. They mean really old people, about eighty, don't they, Mother?'

'I still think you should stay with her, Samantha, just for another couple of nights. She likes having you around. You know I only irritate her. You can have that ice-blue satin blouse in the shop.'

'Bribery and corruption,' said Seb.

His face was asking for a brick. I wrinkled my nose at him to let him know that I thought him pretty disgusting.

I decided to let myself be corrupted. I'd wanted the blouse for a while but Bella had said it was too expensive to let me have.

'Oh, all right! But only two more nights!'

On the second night I couldn't sleep and got up for a drink of water. It was cold in the kitchen. I hugged my dressing-gown round me. Outside, the street looked strange without people around, and only the parked cars standing there. A small shadow moved, low down. Mr Murchie's Tiger, perhaps. Night-time's his time. There was one light on across the road. Maybe someone was ill over there, too. I could hear Granny coughing and wheezing. I went to the door of her room.

'Are you OK, Gran?'

She didn't answer. The wheezing noise was dreadful. I helped her to sit up and put a pillow behind her. She couldn't seem to get her breath properly. I laid her back and ran for the phone.

Mother went with Granny in the ambulance. Seb and I sat huddled in front of the fire in our kitchen and drank coffee. We didn't say much.

'What if – ?' I began, then stopped.

They'd taken her to the City Hospital. Seb and I had wanted to go, too, but there wasn't room in the ambulance. 'One's enough,' the ambulance man had said and closed up the back door, shutting Granny off from our sight. I could still see our mother's ashy white face as she bent over the stretcher.

I kept thinking I could hear the phone but when I went into the hall and looked at it, it was sitting there dead silent. The minutes crawled past. We dozed off. And were jerked awake by the loud ringing of the telephone bell. I dashed into the hall and grabbed the receiver.

'Mum?'

'It's bad. She's got double pneumonia. They say I should come home and they'll call me if necessary.'

Our mother arrived back in a taxi about an hour later. She looked whacked.

'Let's all go to bed,' she said, 'and try to get some sleep. We need to keep our strength up.'

I didn't think I could possibly go to sleep but I must have plummeted straight down like a stone dropping into a well. I woke to find it was midday and couldn't understand what I was doing in bed. I should have been at school. Then I remembered. Granny was ill and might die. No, she wouldn't die, not my granny, she was as strong as a horse, hadn't she often said so herself?

We planned to go and see her in the afternoon but before we could set off the phone rang. It was the hospital to say that Mother should come at once, Granny's condition was critical. We felt stunned. Everything was happening so fast.

Seb called a taxi. We sat, three in a row on the back seat, saying nothing. The city looked odd to me as we swept through it. I felt I'd never seen it properly before. And all those people walking about didn't know what was happening to us.

When we got to the hospital, Mother was whisked off by the matron, and Seb and I were left to sit in a waiting-room. It was hot, and full of people coughing. There were some ratty-looking magazines hanging around but we didn't even feel like picking them up. Seb had his arms folded and his chin was resting on his chest. His eyes were fixed on his knees.

Now I was having to face the idea that Granny *might* die. I'd never thought it could happen before; she wasn't an old granny bent over in the middle, wrapped in shawls, warming herself at the fire all day long. She'd always been out and about and full of vim. (That's what she calls it herself — 'full of vim'.) Remembering her say it made me want to cry. But I mustn't cry, not here in the waiting-room, with all those people staring at me. I'd thought she would go on for ever, or at least for a long time, until I was grown up. I'd *counted* on it. We might grumble about Granny but she's part of our life, and if she went there'd be a hole right in the middle of it.

The door opened, and Bella signalled to us. We went at once.

'Come and sit with me outside her room.'

We sat on a bench and waited again. Hospitals seem to be full of people waiting. Waiting to get better, waiting to die, waiting for appointments, waiting for news. Bella hates waiting for anything, but here she was sitting still as a statue. I knew that, although she and Granny argued a lot, they were really fond of one another underneath.

We sat there for three hours. And then the door opened and a doctor in a white coat came out. We got up. My knees were trembling.

'Is she – ?' My throat felt choked up.

Bella touched my arm.

'She's actually rallied a bit,' said the doctor. 'It's amazing. We thought she was going to go. But *she* didn't seem to think so. She's obviously a fighter.'

'She is that!' said her daughter.

I burst into tears.

The hospital warned us that Granny wasn't out of danger yet, it would be a day or two before they'd know for sure whether she was going to pull through, but, somehow, *we* knew. Once she'd turned that first corner, she'd hang on like grim death. Grim death! She'd been close to it.

Two days later, they were able to take her off oxygen and we were allowed in to see her for a few minutes. She was looking very pale and she'd lost weight, and her hands were lying idle on top of the coverlet. For a moment I didn't recognize her.

In turn, we went to kiss her. Her eyes were wide open and looking at us.

'You gave us a fright there, Mother,' said Bella, sitting herself down on the upright visitor's chair. Seb and I perched on the end of the bed, taking good care not to sit on Granny's feet.

'It'd take more than a wee bit of flu to polish off Ina McKetterick!'

'It was more than flu. You had pneumonia. *Double* pneumonia.'

Granny snorted – just a small snort, but it was a snort nevertheless. A bit of colour was creeping back into her cheeks.

'I'm not ready for the undertaker yet.' She seemed to be getting stronger by the minute. 'I hope you're remembering to feed Charlie?'

'Sam and I are in every day, Gran,' said Seb.

'And my plants?'

'I've given them buckets of water,' I said.

'Not too much, or you'll kill them!'

'They've never looked better.' (That was a lie. The leaves on two of them had turned brown.)

'And mind you double-lock the door when you leave my flat! I'm not wanting burgled while I'm lying in here helpless. Folk are aye ready to take advantage.'

'Looks like she'll soon be back at the nuisance stage,' said our mother, very softly, but not softly enough.

I saw Granny smile.

12

Held in Trust

Seb

I knew that, sooner or later, the family was going to have to face up to the question of what to do about the castle. Our ancestral home! Falling to bits, and leaking like a collander. We'd patched the roof not long ago but you can go on patching old buildings for only so long and then you get to the point when you realize you're going to have to do a thorough overhaul or else you'll have a ruin on your hands. That's what Hari's father, who's an engineer and a practical man, said when I talked it over with him. It looked like we were headed for the ruin scenario.

Our grandfather's Bentley arrived in the street one Saturday afternoon. I had a feeling that it might be him from the sound of the honking horns. He just parks where it takes his fancy, never mind if he's blocking the street. He'd called the night before from a phone box — his telephone had got cut off, he complained, he couldn't think why, though I had an idea. He probably hadn't paid the bill! He'd announced that he had dry rot and then run off without saying where.

I looked down from the window. It was him, sure enough. A taxi driver was hanging out of his cab window and mouthing at him. Three cars were lined up behind the taxi, and all the drivers had their hands on their horns. Grandfather was smiling and waving to the taxi.

'Better go down, Sebastian,' said Bella, 'before we have a riot on our hands.'

I ran down and jumped in beside Grandfather and told him to drive on. We had to go several streets away to find a proper parking space.

'That's what I don't like about the city,' he said. 'In the country we have all the parking spaces in the world.'

We walked back up to the street together.

'About this dry rot, Grandfather?'

He sighed. He doesn't often sigh. 'Mr McKinnon says it's bad.' (Mr Mckinnon is his local builder.) 'The rot's in several lintels, apparently, and the roof rafters. What a nuisance! And there's wet rot in the cellar.'

'The roof's in no great shape, either.'

'What are we to do, Sebastian? Mr McKinnon has given me an estimate. It would cost *hundreds* of thousands.'

We didn't have thousands, never mind hundreds of them.

Torquil came round in the early evening and we had a family powwow. Our grandmother, who was almost back to full strength, joined in, even though, strictly speaking, the castle is no concern of hers. It didn't stop her voicing her opinion, however.

'It'll just have to be sold, there's nothing else for it. If anybody'd buy it,' she added, with a sniff.

We all looked at her with horror. Sell our castle to *strangers*? And never to be able to set foot in it again?

'But it's been in our family for hundreds of years, Mother-in-law,' said Torquil.

'We had to sell *our* family home,' she retorted. (A fisherman's cottage at Newhaven.)

'There *is* a difference.'

'Tell me what then! Just because you think your family's fancier than mine?'

'Now, Mother!' Bella said warningly.

'Now nothing! Some folk don't like to hear the truth.'

'It's just that the castle is a kind of national heritage, Mrs McKetterick,' Grandfather intervened in his most charming and reasonable way. It always disarms Granny. We could do with him around more often.

We reached no conclusions that evening, but the words 'national heritage' started me thinking. When Sam and I went into the kitchen to do the dishes, I said to her, 'Do you remember, when you were in primary school, going to see the Georgian House in Charlotte Square?'

She nodded. 'I liked the way the rooms were all set out like they would have been when it was built.'

'It's run by the National Trust,' I said.

'So?'

'Well, maybe they'd be interested in our castle.'

'To buy, you mean?'

'Wouldn't it be better if they bought it than some stranger? At least then it'd be open to the public and we could still see it.'

'But where would Grandfather live?'

He could hardly live in a caravan in the field. He'd die of hypothermia the first winter. And we don't have enough room in our flat. He'd hate living in the city, anyway.

That evening Viola and I went to Hilary's house to play Trivial Pursuits with her and Hari. I told them about Grandfather's visit and the dry rot.

'I think you'd have to give it to the National Trust,' said Viola, whose parents are members. 'But they usually let the family keep an apartment. And in return you might have to help show the visitors around.'

'Grandfather would enjoy that.' I could see him, wearing the kilt, leading the way down into the dungeons, talking with relish of dark deeds of the past. Could I see myself in the future doing it? I was not so sure. But that would be a long way off, for my father was next in line to inherit, and I could see him doing the showing round bit, *if* he could be relied upon to be there.

'Why don't you go and talk to them at the Georgian House?' suggested Hari.

Sam and I decided to go on Monday, after school. Hari volunteered (after I'd twisted his arm) to do the paper round. I put on my sports jacket and Sam wore her best coat. Bella was in the shop so she didn't see us and ask what we were doing all dressed up. We didn't want to say anything to anyone else in the family until we'd done our initial recce.

We walked uptown to the West End and turned into Charlotte Square. It's a big, stately square, and the façades are imposing. The Secretary of State for Scotland has his official residence there, at number six.

'I feel nervous, Seb.' Sam was walking so close to me she was kicking me in the ankle. 'Don't you? Maybe they'll think we've got an awful cheek.'

'We can only ask.' I didn't feel as confident as I might have sounded. But what was there to lose? We could only be sent off with a flea in our ear. (Oh yes, that's a Granny expression!)

We went up the steps of number seven. The heavy front door was firmly closed. The house was not open to the public in February. I hesitated for a second, then pulled the brass bell.

After a moment we heard footsteps. The door opened,

and a lady looked out at us.

'Hello.' She sounded friendly. 'Can I help you?'

'We've got this castle,' said Sam in a rush. She always has to open up her mouth and let everything tumble out.

'A castle?'

'Yes, it belongs to our grandfather. It's in Argyll.'

'I see.'

'We think we might like to give it to you.'

'Well, in that case perhaps you should come in.'

We were about to follow her in when we heard someone calling us. '*Sam and Seb!*' We turned. There, on the pavement, stood our grandmother. She'd been told by the doctor to get out and about more, take some exercise. So here she was taking it.

'Granny!' bleated Sam, like a sick lamb.

'What in the name are you two up to, would you tell me?'

'Is this your grandmother?' asked the National Trust lady. 'In that case, maybe she'd like to come in too?'

As the saying goes – there's no show without Punch. Punch came up the steps and went sailing through the hall of the Georgian House with us trailing in her wake eyeing one another and making faces.

The woman took us into a little room which seemed to be her office. She fetched another couple of chairs and we all sat down, with her behind the desk and the three of us in a row with Granny in the middle. Talk about having a spanner thrown into the works! It felt more like a sledgehammer. I'd rehearsed with Hari beforehand what we should say; now I couldn't remember a word of it.

'So – you've got a castle you might want to give to us?'

123

'That's what you're doing here then, is it?' interrupted Granny, swivelling first to look at me and then Sam. 'But what's this about *give*? If we're going to be doing anything, it'll be selling.'

'Granny,' I said, feeling my face getting hotter by the second, 'the National Trust doesn't often buy properties. It couldn't afford to. People usually give them to them.'

'More fool them!'

'They give them in trust for the nation.' I wished we could make our escape, but here we were all packed in sitting elbow to elbow like sardines. Dislodging Granny would be like trying to prise a limpet from a rock.

'Why don't you tell me the whole story?' said the woman, who probably thought we were all nuts but was being terribly polite.

So we did, Sam laying on the full horror of the dry rot etc. in gory detail, with me trying to play it down. The woman listened closely, nodding from time to time, as if she had possibly heard it all before.

'Well, I have to say that I am very sympathetic,' she said, when we'd finished. 'I'm sure it must be a terrible drain trying to keep up a castle.'

'A *drain*?' echoed Granny. 'It's like pouring water through a sieve putting money into yon place. The roof itself's got as many holes as a sieve. More!' I tried to dunt her in the side but she wasn't paying any attention, she was launched on one of her favourite topics. 'The building's like an ice box even in the middle of summer. You'd need to be an Eskimo to put up with yon. It's not *my* castle, you understand. It's their grandfather's on their *father's* side.' The way she said 'father' made him sound like a first degree murderer. I wanted to strangle her.

Then Sam decided to put her oar in. 'So do you think

you might be interested in having it?' she asked, looking
the National Trust woman straight in the eye, as if she
expected her to give an answer on the spot when she
hadn't even seen the place. They'd have to send surveyors and lawyers to look at it first, and goodness
knows who else!

'It's possible that we *could* be interested. We don't
have too much property in Argyll.'

Sam sat back, smiling, as if that was that.

'But there is one big problem, which you may not
have thought of.'

We waited. There's always a problem, no matter what
you're trying to do.

'Money.'

'We know,' said Sam. 'That's why we've come to you.'

'Yes, but you see, we don't take on properties unless
there's some kind of endowment fund to go with them
to help pay for repairs and upkeep.'

'How much would you be talking about?' I asked.

'Difficult to say offhand. But probably something over
a million.'

'A million *pounds*?' Granny trumpeted. 'If we'd a
million pounds you wouldn't see us for dust!'

Afterwards, we went to McDonald's, Granny too, and
had hamburgers and Coke to cheer ourselves up. Well,
so much for my bright idea!

'A million *pounds*!' said Sam, taking a bite of her
burger. 'Where could we get that? We don't know any
millionaires.'

'Yes, we do!' said Granny. 'What about Ollie? The
Yank. Your American cousin twice removed, or whatever he's supposed to be. He paid for yon roof bill. There
may be more where that came from.'

'Granny,' I said, 'sometimes you do have good ideas!'

'Why would he want to give us a million pounds?' asked Sam.

'We couldn't expect him to give *us* a million pounds but he might be prepared to give it to the National Trust.'

'But why?'

'To save the family seat. Americans are keen on things like that.' (As are we.)

'You write to him, son, when we go home and put it to him. There's no harm in trying.' Granny downed the last of her Coke. 'You get nowhere in this life without chancing your arm once in a while.'

But 'mum' was the word, we agreed; we'd keep it to ourselves until we'd sounded Ollie out.

We had to wait two weeks for a reply. Every time Granny came in she'd look at me meaningfully and raise her eyebrow and I'd shake my head.

When Ollie did write he said that he *might* be prepared to help, with the word 'might' underlined. He would have to know a great deal more about it, of course. And then he would consider coming over.

'Right then,' said Granny, 'now's the time to let everyone else in on it.'

'Well, well!' said Torquil sarcastically. 'You have been busy, haven't you, the three of you?' And he looked at Granny.

'Don't blame Gran!' I jumped in quickly. 'It was my idea.'

'I don't mind being *blamed*! We were just trying to help, to get *you* out of a hole, Torquil!' Our grandmother was waxing indignant.

'I wasn't aware of *being* in a hole, Mother-in-law!'

'Yon castle's nothing but a heap of holes. Or will be if you don't do something about it soon.'

'Don't let's start an argument!' I pleaded.

Now my grandmother looked annoyed at me, as if I'd accused her of starting it. Our family is hopeless when it comes to trying to have a reasonable discussion. And our mother was sulking because we hadn't let her in on our secret before.

'Talk about sneaky kids! *And* a sneaky grandmother!'

I suggested we ring Grandfather, who said he'd be over the next day. Clementina, on hearing the news, dropped her sweaters and the Flowers and *flew* down from Orkney. She was in a great tizzy.

'The very *idea* of giving our castle away! How could you even *consider* it? It's my home too, you know!'

'You're hardly ever there,' said Torquil. 'Once a year in the summer for a couple of weeks.'

'We spent a month there last year, didn't we, Father? The Flowers *adore* it.' (They'd just about given everyone a heart attack by playing at tight-rope walkers on the parapet ledge.) 'And how often are *you* there, brother dear?'

After a bit more along those lines, Granny banged on the table with a spoon. 'Now then, let's get down to business! We'll never get anywhere at this rate.'

By this time Torquil had come round to the idea of the National Trust. As he'd said to us, when our grandfather died (which wouldn't be for a very long time, we hoped) we'd have to sell the castle to pay the taxes. And by then Ollie might have changed his mind about the million, or lost all his money. And as Granny had said, you've got to strike when the iron is hot.

'I think it's a *terrible* idea.' Clementina was not going to give up. 'I'd rather it was a semi-ruin but still ours.

You'd hate people trampling all over it, wouldn't you, Father? Hundreds and hundreds of people in tackity boots and dripping macs.'

'Can't say I've ever fancied the idea much.'

'They'd drop crisp packets and Coke cans in the grounds – '

'What grounds?' demanded Granny.

'And buses would be parked outside the front door.'

'Buses?' said Grandfather. 'I couldn't have that. I hate buses. Noisy things.'

'Belching out fumes,' said Clementina. 'Polluting the atmosphere.'

'They wouldn't have to come *right* up to the front door,' said Torquil.

'It would only be for half the year,' I pointed out. 'And maybe only afternoons, from two to five.'

'*Every* afternoon though, Father, right through the summer.'

And so it went on, for hours. In the end Grandfather said sadly – and then I felt miserable – that he supposed he would have to move with the times. 'When the cash runs out you've got to be realistic. And I must say it would be nice to see the old place spruced up again. Think of it that way, Clementina – we'll be giving it a new lease of life.'

We didn't manage to change Clementina's mind. But she was outvoted. She flew back to Orkney after calling us all a list of unprintable names.

The Trust went ahead and sent in surveyors and curators. Then Ollie arrived and further hectic activity ensued at Charlotte Square and in Argyll. Sam and I were on tenterhooks the whole time, well aware that at any point the whole thing could fall through. The Trust might decide against it, or Ollie might find it was going to cost too much.

When he was over in Argyll with the surveyors, we rang up Grandfather twice a day. (His phone had been reinstated.) We didn't learn much.

'They're crawling over every single inch. They're being very thorough, I must say.'

'Goodness knows what they're finding!' said Granny, uttering all our fears. 'The mind boggles.'

Then Grandfather rang to tell us that the surveyors had given the thumbs up. Ollie returned, and disappeared into the National Trust's headquarters to talk money. After that, our application had to be considered and approved by the Trust's Council.

On the day of their meeting we waited at home for Ollie to bring back the news. Hari and Hilary and Viola were there, too, and Morag dropped in as well.

'I feel sick,' Sam said. 'The excitement's killing me.'

The time crawled past slowly.

Then the doorbell rang, and in came Ollie carrying a magnum of champagne! He was smiling.

'Well, that's it, folks – it's all ready to be signed, sealed and delivered! And the family will have its apartment so you don't need to worry about your grandad.'

For a moment I wanted to cheer, along with the others. Then I realized what it actually meant. If the National Trust *was* going to take over the castle it wouldn't be *ours* any longer. We'd be allowed the use of the apartment, but wouldn't own it. The castle had been ours for a long time, over three hundred years. We'd groaned over it, moaned about its leaking roof and freezing passages, called it a millstone round our necks, but we'd loved it. I felt myself go quiet. The kind of holidays that we'd had would be over. We could still go of course, but it wouldn't be the same, we'd be confined to a small part, and there'd be tourists traipsing about, gaping at our family portraits, eating their sandwiches on the rocks. We didn't *have* to go through with it, we could still pull back. It wasn't signed and sealed yet. Maybe I'd made a terrible mistake by starting the whole thing off. I hadn't thought through all the implications.

Ollie eased out the champagne cork. We stood in a circle and raised our glasses. Ollie made the toast.

'Well, here's to the castle's new era!'

We drank.

'The Scottish Tourist Board is going to give us a grant for the shop,' said Ollie. 'So that's good news.'

'The *shop*?' I repeated.

'They always have shops at these places, Sebastian,' said Bella. 'They sell souvenirs, tea cloths, soap, shortbread, that kind of thing.'

'It brings in extra income, and it's another attraction,' said Ollie, who was now an expert on the Stately Homes business. Though I couldn't see our castle qualifying as being 'stately'!

'There'll be a tea-room as well.'

'A *tea-room*?' said Sam. 'Gosh, I never imagined all these things. Shops and tea-rooms!'

'Sounds a bit like Blackpool,' I commented. The champagne tasted bitter in my mouth.

'Blackpool!' Granny was scornful. 'The day yon place resembles Blackpool I'll eat my hat!'

'Hey, you could help run the tea-room, Gran,' said Sam.

'Or act as a guide, Mother-in-law,' put in Torquil. 'Show the people round.'

'I daresay I could if I'd a mind to.' My grandmother drained her glass and held it out for a refill. Port was her preferred tipple, but champagne would do nicely.

Torquil came over to join me. He raised his glass to mine. 'Our castle has had a long and varied history, son. So now it's going to enter a new era. And new eras are often painful, at least to begin with. But let's drink to it!' We clinked glasses. 'It has to be, Seb, we both know that. We couldn't have let it go on as it was. The only way we can give it a chance to survive is by handing it over to the nation to be held in trust.'

I nodded. He was right: there was no going back.

When we rang Grandfather to tell him the news, he said, 'So be it. As long as they let me keep my Aga! And I daresay some of the people will be rather nice.'

Granny, of course, has to be allowed to have the last word.

As she sipped her champagne she was warming to the idea of being a castle guide. To have a posse of people under her control would suit her down to the ground, as she herself might put it.

'I think I'd be equipped for the job. For a start, I'd be able to tell them a thing or two about the family history that'd make their hair curl!' She looked round at us all. We straightened up and tried to look innocent. But Granny is not easily fooled. She nodded. 'Aye, there's plenty I could tell them about this family — past *and* present!'

Also in Puffin

ESIO TROT
Roald Dahl

Mr Hoppy is in love with Mrs Silver. But Mrs Silver has eyes only for Alfie, her pet tortoise. How can he ever compete with such a rival? He comes up with a bold plan to win his lady's love, involving some clever riddles and a whole army of tortoises. Will Mr Hoppy's patience be rewarded? And what's to become of Alfie?

A highly comic and unusual love story.

JUST FERRET
Gene Kemp

Owen Hardacre, otherwise known as Ferret, has been dragged around the country by his artist father and been to so many schools that he doesn't expect much from Cricklepit Combined School. But when he makes friends with Beany and Minty and gains the respect of Sir, things begin looking up . . . even the reading!

Meet Ferret, his friends *and* enemies in this fifth story of the pupils of Cricklepit Combined School.

DID YOU THINK I WOULD LEAVE YOU CRYING?
Moira Miller

This collection of sensitive and moving stories traces the effects of conflict and compassion across the years; the friendship, the heroism and the cruelty of war.

MAN IN MOTION
Jan Mark

Once Lloyd has started at his new school, he soon finds he's playing cricket with Salman, swimming with Kenneth, cycling with James and playing badminton with Vlad. But American football is Lloyd's greatest enthusiasm. And in time it tests his loyalties, not only to his other sporting activities, but also to the new friends he shares them with.

THE OUTSIDE CHILD
Nina Bawden

Imagine suddenly discovering you have a step-brother and -sister no one has ever told you about! It's the most exciting thing that's ever happened to Jane, and she can't wait to meet them. Perhaps at last she will become part of a 'proper' family, instead of forever being the outside child. So begins a long search for her brother and sister, but when she finally does track them down, Jane finds there are still more surprises in store!

THE FOX OF SKELLAND
Rachel Dixon

Samantha's never liked the old custom of Foxing Day – the fox costume especially gives her the creeps. So when Jason and Rib, children of the new publicans at The Fox and Lady, find the costume and Jason wears it to the fancy-dress disco, she's sure something awful will happen.

Then Sam's old friend Joseph sees the ghost of the Lady and her fox. Has she really come back to exact vengeance on the village? Or has her appearance got something to do with the spate of burglaries in the area?